The Last Generation

The Lie About Coming-of-Age Stories

D1738402

J.T. Wilkinson

Table of Contents

Introduction

Consider me a time traveler. I exist without a physical form, considering that I have no tangible presence. I am occupying that space in your head, allowing me to borrow your voice. I'm curious. Whose voice do you hear in your mind when reading this? This is the power of those who write. We can enter your most personal space, a realm even your closest loved ones cannot penetrate. Your mind. But what is this internal dialogue really? That space defines our humanity, shaping who we are as humans. A soul? Consciousness? Or is it merely data that can be transferred and stored? At this moment, how connected are you with your inner self? Think about what defines you for a moment. Your home, your career, your future goals, your family, the love of your life, your sadness, or if you even will make it to the next day. Are you certain this is who you are and who you will continue to be? Incorrect. Whatever you said. Wherever you are in your life right now. Wrong. As a time traveler from the future, I can confidently tell you that is not the case. I understand that you may have countered this in your mind and engaged in a mental debate, but remember, I am not physically present, so you are essentially debating with yourself. Have you ever been so happy, so overjoyed with life that you were certain, so certain this is how your life would be like? If you are sitting there at a point in your life where you can't answer. You are not lost. Your feelings are not wrong. In fact, I want you to embrace them. All of them. The love of that holiday town you visited, wishing to move there. Your first true love. The passion for a new hobby. The feeling of the first day of your new job. Those certainties are real. And when you find yourself uncertain about these things, that's when I want you to know that I'm certain you are exactly where you need to be. Is certainty doomed to follow an inverse path with time? Or is there some singularity, some event that can change that? Your life is not one love story waiting to happen; it's a beautiful collection of love stories and experiences that create something so unique, that there is only one being that can create that complex data like a snowflake falling to the Earth: YOU. Your soul is not a linear path from birth to death. Think of it more as a seed growing into a beautiful tree. And with every new experience, every new love, every fallen leaf, every loss you go through, these gardeners of your soul teach you to love better, to give more, to be more of yourself, what you like and don't like, bringing you closer to realizing you are exactly who you are supposed to be. You just might not have bloomed yet.

Chapter 1

Liam was seated on the edge of his bed, gazing out the window at the sunset. The hues on the Tahoe trees were stunning, and he felt as though he was standing in front of a divine painting. Dew sparkles on the foliage, creating hundreds of diamonds that decorate the cabin. Although he had spent part of his summer there before, that day seemed particularly special. Liam was lost in the moment, taking in the birdsongs, the smell of wet grass, and the sunbeam that's focused on the bed where Sarah lay asleep. My stomach was all twisted with nerves—that day, he would pop the question.

He looked over to check the time on the clock: 6 a.m. He turned back to Sarah and stared admiringly at her long, blonde hair reflecting light. Her hazel eyes were revealed when she stirred awake.

"What are you doing, weirdo?" she said, her arms stretching while some blankets fell away to reveal her bare chest. "Come close the blinds and get back into bed!"

Liam rose from the bed, closed the curtains, and then returned to it.

"Sorry, I couldn't sleep," he said as he crawled back in beside her. She opened her arms and welcomed him into the embrace of her body, murmuring, "Just a couple more hours." He nestled between her legs, as his chest rested against her hip, and his head found its place on her chest with an ear pressed to her heart. His skin felt delicate beneath her touch, yet each contact sent electricity coursing through him like a jolt of energy. One arm held him close while the other caressed his hair. He wanted to pause time so this moment would last forever, but the minutes continued to pass until he drifted off to sleep again.

When Liam awoke an hour later, he carefully got out of bed without disturbing her slumber. He pulled on a pair of gray sweatpants that were lying by the foot of the bed and kicked his discarded clothing from the night before into a pile. He grabbed the two empty wine glasses and bottle that had been left on the nightstand, along with a card that read, "Happy three-year anniversary."

He headed to the kitchen and tossed the empty bottles away. Simple things always made her happy, so Liam decided to prepare breakfast. The bacon was gorgeous: Perfect slices of meat that came off the stove still a little pink and bleeding. The eggs were fluffy, and the yolks were firm, not runny. The coffee was steaming, sitting in an old-fashioned ceramic mug. It tasted strong and creamy, but not bitter; the espresso and sugar were sweet on their own, but complemented the coffee instead of overcompensating for its bitterness. It was thick and creamy; a cream-colored foam as white as the clouds in the sky. It could have been a sky full of clouds instead of white foam, but the sky wasn't white. It was blue. A light blue, like the color of the ocean. The eggs looked like a great mountain range with little bumps in the center, like rocky peaks in the sand. The bacon was crunchy, like the sound of the ocean waves crashing against the rocks or the sand, and cut into little pieces, like the shape of fish scales

Liam was not one for breakfast foods. Even if he was, that combo would be a strange choice. He'd settle for a good BLT instead. Sourdough bread, fresh tomatoes, and thick, crispy bacon—that's his idea of a perfect meal. But that day was all about her. He cooked the bacon first and put on some extra strips, so he could snack on it while preparing the rest of the meal. As breakfast neared completion, he took out his phone and put on some music from her favorite artist to set the mood—something she loved when waking up in the mornings. Liam put on some music that would help them both relax: Mozart's Requiem in D minor. Yes, it's morbid music for mornings, but they're not normal people.

"I smell bacon," Sarah announced as she casually walked into the kitchen, still wearing his shorts and hoodie. Her long, blonde hair was pulled back into a bun that reached down to her shoulders. Although petite, she exuded confidence like no other.

Liam towered over her at 6'1", but the sight of her made him grin ear to ear like an idiot. She started talking, but he didn't hear a word she said.

Focus, Liam. Nod your head and pay attention. Suddenly, she jumped on him, and he caught her in his arms—one of his favorite greetings. Their embrace was so close that Liam could feel her heart beating against his. She grabbed his face and looked at him in the eye with a smile.

"Are you listening to me?" she asked teasingly.

"Huh, sorry. Can't blame me, coming in here looking like that," he said to dodge the question.

"Wait, the bacon! Put me down!" she spoke.

She was light as a feather. Liam carried her over to the kitchen counter and put her down on top near the plate of bacon. As she started to munch on the bacon strips, he grabbed a plate of runny eggs and a cup of coffee and brought the plate over to her. He just smiled and watched as she did her happy food dance sitting on the counter. It's definitely the simple things.

She caught him gawking. "What?!" she barked at him.

"Nothing," he replied with a shrug. "Excited for our hike?"

In an instant, her anticipation of the hike was supplanted by hunger as she hopped off the counter to get something to eat.

Meanwhile, Liam busied himself with tidying up and packing the truck. He made sure to include in his backpack an extra bottle of water, a camera, and, of course, the ring. Although they were still young, Liam could no longer wait to start the next chapter of their lives together—he was sure that they were meant to be soulmates.

They drove south to Maggie's Peak Trail. When you reach its peak, you are about 1900 feet above elevation, and then you can gaze out upon the stunning blue lake, the mountain capped with snow even on hot days, and the lush green trees that encompass it all. That hike had become like an annual ritual for them; nothing too strenuous, but still a good workout. Afterward, they pampered themselves with a decadent dinner and drinks.

He arrived at the parking lot with Sarah earlier than usual, hoping to find a spot for the two of them in private. They encountered a couple walking their little Golden poodle, and Sarah's attention was diverted away from Liam. He checked his backpack once more for the ring, just to make sure it was still there. Then, she came running towards him, eager for kisses. For a few seconds, the sky grew dark as if a passerby had snuffed out the sun—yet, there was no clouds in sight.

"What are you staring at? What's up with you today? Did you smoke something?" Sarah teased him.

They hiked up the trail, the time going by so quickly as They chatted. They'd known each other for three years, and it still seemed like he could keep listening to her stories for hours. Her passion for life and her goals came through in her words. They took time along the way to take pictures of creeks and waterfalls. As they made their way toward the summit, his palms sweated, although Liam wasn't sure if it was from nerves or fatigue. Fortunately, she didn't notice.

He paused and surveyed the landscape. A creek carved a path between rocks at the summit, so Liam hopped down to get closer to it. Reaching out to touch the water, he couldn't even feel it—or its temperature—anymore. Was his hand numb? No... He remembered it being cold. Why did he have such a strange sense of déjà vu? Liam reached for a water bottle in his pack, assuming dehydration was the cause of his confusion, while he still took in the scenery.

And there it was, the perfect spot. A rock big enough to sit on, with a clear view of the lake. Where the blue water and sky blurred together in the sun's brilliance. She perched upon the rock, taking a sip from her water bottle as Liam knelt down. Her figure silhouetted by the sun, looking almost angelic.

He was reminded of that first winter they had spent together; when he had too much wine one night and revealed his sappy playlist. The song was "Hanging by a Moment". Liam remembered turning red, feeling embarrassed as she saw what he'd hidden away. Yet, she simply smiled back at him, saying "I love Life House". That moment felt like his heart was beating for the very first time. They danced together under the moonlight; he hadn't felt that warmth with anyone else before.

"My love. It didn't come from looks, or even intelligence. You've done more for me in these three years than you can ever know, and when I stare into your eyes, I feel safe. All I want to do is make you happy for the rest of your life. I promise to give each day to you, Sarah. Will you marry me?"

Liam's heart leaped with joy as she nodded her head and put her hand to her mouth. He felt tears streaming down his face, but didn't realize he was crying. He, then, slipped the ring onto her finger and they both watched it glint in the sunlight. Liam wished that moment would never end.

But, then, something strange happened: the world suddenly stopped around them. The wind ceased, and all movement froze. Liam tried to move, but couldn't—it was as if he'd been paralyzed. His breathing became frantic, yet he couldn't feel his body's motion. All sound faded away, except for the thumping of his heart that was so loud it sounded like a drum being banged on. He could no longer look down at his hands; everything became darker and darker until all that remained was darkness and his thoughts, which were quickly fading too. No... Stop... Sarah...

Chapter 2

It's not easy to predict what the future holds. In 1970, people were certain the 2000s would bring us futuristic flying cars and a lifestyle like The Jetsons. In 2000, they thought our world would be overrun by advanced artificial intelligence, or we'd have to endure dystopic civilizations. In 2030, they figured we'd destroy Earth by 2060 with an asteroid-induced apocalypse or WWIII. But none of that happened. What did happen are the slow and subtle changes in how we interact with one another. We act with more kindness towards our townsfolk and neighbors, regardless of origin or political persuasion. We strive for equality and justice for those who are disadvantaged. Yes, technology advances rapidly, but underlying it all are core values from when humans first formed tribes. Let's look at San Francisco in 2104: Buildings still exist, but now they're taller, sturdier, and better for the environment. Cars still run, but on cleaner fuel sources. Yet relics from the past remain in place, too—like Fenway Park sitting alongside new construction. This is what life looks like when the past meets the present: you can find the Golden Gate Bridge standing as a relic of old engineering surrounded by the Presidio's lush green pastures that existed long before Spanish colonization began in 1776. On the other side of town, massive skyscrapers tower over the city, casting shadows in every direction; these sky-high residences and corporate buildings filled San Francisco when its population increased drastically, requiring people to make adjustments in order to survive. You can even find entire neighborhoods where groceries, dentist offices, gyms, entertainment centers, and housing all occupy the same floor. Our story begins at one of these skyscrapers in downtown San Francisco, where Liam woke up after blacking out 80 years ago.

Liam opened his eyes to a blinding white scene. His neck was stiff like he had been sleeping for days. He quickly noticed the stark, sterile room: nothing but white walls and flooring. He lay in an exam chair with an IV connected to him, bandages wrapped around his head. He had no recollection of how he got there or what happened prior. On the desk was a tablet, and Liam could hear people talking outside the door about him waking up and asking for someone named Tithonus.

A series of quick, frantic footsteps reverberated along the hallway in a rhythm. Boom. Boom. Boom. The rhythm was broken by a louder, heavier footstep that got closer to the door.

"How long has he been awake? Has anyone gone in there before me? Does the board know?" a male voice asked. "Good."

Knock. Knock. Knock. The door opened, and Liam saw an unexpected figure: a tall, muscular man with black skin and wavy black hair, blue eyes, and a sharp jawline; he looked like he could star in an action movie, rather than be a doctor.

"Liam," he said. "I'm Dr. Tithonus. May I come in and have a chat?"

Liam, scared but eager for answers, nodded as the man stepped inside, towering above him in his white lab coat.

Dr. Tithonus took out a notepad and sighed as he spoke again. "Now, I know you must have questions—"

"Where's Sarah? Is she hurt?" Liam interrupted anxiously.

The doctor looked puzzled, "Sarah? Who is that?"

"My fiancé! I was with her and then... and then... I don't remember what happened next. I woke up here."

Dr. Tithonus furrowed his brows while taking notes. "So, your last memory was with this woman called Sarah? Alright, Liam, listen closely. I need to explain some things to you, and it's going to be quite hard to hear. So, we'll take it step by step, okay?"

Liam felt his heart racing—something had happened to Sarah; that much he knew already. *Oh God, did they fall off the cliff!?* he thought.

"So, let's start with today's date. It's December 5, 2104. Can you guess what day it is?"

Liam was immediately thrown off; yesterday had been the summer of 2024, from his perspective. He stuttered a baffled "what?"

The doctor chuckled before saying, "I'm not sure how to explain this. Maybe I should just show you." He gestured towards one of the plain white walls in the room. Liam must have had an incredulous expression on his face because the doctor smiled at him knowingly before nodding towards the right wall.

Liam's expression dropped as he absentmindedly moved from the chair towards what used to be a wall, now replaced with an eight-foot window overlooking the skyline. He took in his surroundings: tall buildings everywhere and people down below looking like ants. On the distant horizon was an ocean with boats sailing in the harbor, creating a feeling of familiarity. He scanned his surroundings desperately searching for clues of what city he was in, and then his eyes locked onto a small pyramid-like building, which he instantly recognized as the TransAmerica Building in San Francisco. His memories began flooding him with brief images of when he was young—jogging across the Golden

Gate Bridge each morning until fate had him trip right in front of a blonde tourist, Sarah, who nursed his twisted ankle at a nearby café.

Liam stared at Tithonus in disbelief.

"It's real," the doctor insisted. He motioned for Liam to put his hand out.

Confused, Liam had to ask him to repeat himself. "Pardon?"

"From where you are standing, stretch your arm out. Go ahead." He pointed at his own hand for emphasis.

Liam obeyed, and suddenly realized he could feel air on his fingertips; he heard a soft wind too. How was that possible?

He then felt something solid appear in the same place he'd just stretched his hand out— but he didn't see the doctor press any buttons or do anything else.

"How did you—"

Tithonus smiled. "The window rolled itself down. Technology can be quite helpful if you use it right. It's so clear that you can't tell where the edge of the glass starts or ends! Be careful when you reach out again, though. You can pull your arm back in now."

Liam followed his advice and looked up with wonder.

He, then, glanced away, and the wall was back to its ordinary white color.

"Liam... No, you did not time travel, but this is still the future. It's possible because your consciousness can be downloaded and even saved: that concept existed even when you were young. My company made it a reality, and with great success, it worked very well in all the first trials. Our trust in it grew, which is how I ended up here like you. But that same confidence led us to some problems. We followed all protocols, yet we had an unexpected power outage that disrupted the process for Liam's data by a millisecond; less than a quarter of his data got uploaded correctly, while the originals were corrupted. How old do you think you are?" Tithonus asked.

"Twenty-five," Liam replied without hesitation.

Tithonus looked at him with regret in his eyes. "Liam, you had lived a wonderful life until you were 105 years old. You are the fourth volunteer we had for this process, and should have waited before doing yours as the last one... But unfortunately, a millisecond without power is all it took."

"How is this possible?" Liam said incredulously.

"Well, it all goes back to the era we call the Illumination, when scientists managed to unlock more of their brains. Just a small percentage was enough; like switching on a lightbulb and—" the doctor began to explain.

"No, not that," Liam interrupted. "What happened to me?"

"For you, think of it like everything after turning twenty-five years old is gone. You're essentially twenty-five again. But don't worry, we're doing our best to bring your memories back," the doctor spoke slowly, trying to be reassuring.

Liam started to pace back and forth as he muttered: "Again?! This is my first time. No, this can't be real."

He looked up in hope as the doctor continued: "Liam, take a moment to process this. I know this must be difficult for you, but trust me, I'll do whatever it takes to get your memories back. I've contacted your family so that they can help jog some of your lost memories, maybe spark something."

The word "family" gave him a sliver of relief, which was quickly replaced with fear—what family? His mum? His dad? He almost asked if they were alive, then stopped himself. He wanted to cling on to a tiny bit of hope that his mother would walk through those doors laughing and telling him this was all just some sick joke.

"Send him in," the doctor murmured towards thin air.

A man walked into the room, and he wasn't Liam's mum. He was probably in his sixties and had salt-and-pepper hair, wore a San Diego Forty Niners hoodie and skinny jeans (which no old man should ever wear), and sandals, like a scrawny stoner version of Liam's dad.

The man glared at Dr. Tithonus with displeasure and then glanced at Liam. His expression changed as he realized who Liam was. I'm his *dad?* Liam thought, stunned by this new information.

"Liam, I must stress how important it is for you to know what I am about to say next. We are working on getting your memories back, but only have a brief period of time before the likelihood of recovery plummets," declared Dr. Tithonus.

The man shifted his attention back to the doctor. "How much time? Weeks? Months?" he asked.

"Three days," replied the doctor.

The man yelled in anger, "Three days! How can this be possible? Look what you did to him! I have to look after my—"

A loud ringing pounded Liam's ear as information overwhelmed him. He couldn't remember how much longer the other two talked, only that he blankly left the office. Now, standing next to him, was a total stranger in an elevator, taking him to some foreign place, where even more unknowable faces were supposedly his family. He stood there and focused on the top number: three hundred and two. *That's a very tall building*, he thought. Then, his gaze dropped to fifty, then the middle number one, and finally landed on that lit-up button labeled "G." All the numbers melted into the walls and the doors opened. Liam hesitated for a second, as if searching for some other route, but after gathering himself, he stepped out of the elevator, followed by this man, who he now knew was his "son". As he emerged into the hall, a guard jostled him roughly, startling him back into reality. *Armed men still exist today*, Liam thought. Some future.

A rectangle glowed on the ground, though there were no light fixtures illuminating it. Liam and his son marveled at the sight as they approached and saw a couple, both dressed in business clothes, standing in the box of light. There was total silence, but when Liam looked over at them, their faces were expressionless and glassy. Then suddenly, a loud "HA HA" rang out and startled him. His son explained that they weren't just standing there; rather, they were communicating... Like texting on a phone, but without needing to vocalize it.

Liam looked back and noticed that they made faces—squinting eyes, scowling brows— just like he did when messaging people on his phone.

The car had a mirror finish and in the reflection, Liam saw himself, his son, and the businessman reflected on the side of the car. It looked like they were in a hallway looking at it. As he looked on, the car seemed to rise off the ground like a magic trick and hover for a few seconds before the side door whooshed open.

The businessman's eyes were dark, as if they were missing something. His face was ashen, made whiter by the glare of the sun. His hair was whitish gray and cut short.

The car was seamless, like a giant piece of chocolate. It had no headlights, no engine, no reflectors, not an airbag in sight. It floated on the road, moving closer and closer with a soft hum that faded farther than you could see. Liam could not see a driver.

"You're a real hoot, Tiff. See you tomorrow," the man said as he climbed into the car, the door lid opening and closing with a vertical motion. The woman, still gazing at the parking lot, replied softly, "Yeah, see you then."

Liam didn't see the man hop in the driver's seat, nor did he see a driver, but the car took off anyways. *Huh, must be self-driving cars*, he picked up quickly. That's not too surprising, they were working on that during his time too.

The next car that pulled up was a bit bigger, like an SUV, but it looked more like a turtle shell. Gray, with just one door in the center.

"That's us," his son exclaimed as he ducked his head and stepped into the car. It had leather seats lined around the inside in a horseshoe shape—a look that reminded him of a limousine.

"Hello, where do you wish to go?" said a calm and soothing British voice from somewhere in the vehicle.

"I messed with some settings and set it to have this British accent," he said jokingly, as if embarrassed he got caught, even though Liam hadn't asked anything. "Athanasia Complex Presidio, San Francisco, California, please," his son replied. Liam wasn't sure what the first word meant, but he remembered the Presidio of San Francisco.

The car started driving off and out of the parking garage into an enormous underground tunnel—like a highway without a sky. As soon as they reached their destination, the windows tinted black.

"Presidio? Is that where you live?"

"Oh, no," the man shook his head. "The company who messed all this up is called Athanasia... stupid name, I know. But no, I live in San Diego."

Liam nodded his head in understanding. "Ah, that explains the shirt."

The man smiled slightly before continuing. "Ya 49ers! Damn, we were so close this year too... If it weren't for those stupid Vancouver Seahawks, we would've won the World Bowl!"

As Liam listened, he began to realize that he was not on his own timeline. He glanced out the window, even though he could not see through it. He replayed the moment when the man who supposedly was his son walked into the doctor's office—it felt like it all happened in a flash, though hours had passed. He recalled the man didn't look at Liam again after introducing himself as his son. Instead, the man became like a time bomb and the doctor seemed to be part of a bomb squad trying to figure out which wire to cut without setting it off.

Liam pieced together some of what was said: lots of legal jargon about suing and fixing the problem. It didn't matter to him, there was only one thing he wanted to know: Where was Sarah? Then he realized that if this person was truly his son, then he must know her name.

Back in the car, hope shined in Liam's eyes as he turned toward the man and asked, "You're my son?"

"Supposedly. This is all very strange to me."

"So. That means I got married. Had a kid. Maybe kids. So, where is Sarah?"

"Who?"

"My wife. Your mom."

"Dad. Mom's name is Emily... I don't know any Sarah."

This new information sent Liam into a fit of rage and confusion, and he started hyperventilating. "Wrong! Wrong, wrong, wrong! You're lying! Where am I? Why are you doing this to me?"

His son put his hands up in a gesture of surprise, asking "Dad?"

"Don't touch me! Don't call me Dad. Stop. This is too much. Pull over so I can get out."

"Calm down. We can't do that," exclaimed the dad.

Liam searched for door handles, but there were none—he felt more and more trapped by the moment.

"Let me out! Please, please!" begged Liam. He was becoming increasingly frantic and began to demand the car comply. "Lower the tint!" The windows darkened before fading back to clear glass from the side windows to the roof, revealing they were still underground, surrounded by hundreds of cars barely moving, although Liam could tell from the tunnel lights that they were going faster than ever before.

"See, we can't stop, but we will be there soon. Just calm down and we'll figure this out. I knew it wasn't a good idea," said the son.

"Where are you taking me? Why there? You said you don't live there."

"The Presidio... They have housing there. It's basically a place where they will look after you for the next three days until they sort this out."

"I don't want to go there."

"Well, yeah, do you think I *want* to fucking be here? It was *your* idea." His son was clearly getting frustrated by now. "At least you'll get to see the kids and Andrew."

"I don't know who Andrew is or who these kids are."

"Yeah, well, you never seemed to know them anyway."

Liam felt terrible without understanding why. He stopped talking in an effort to regain his composure, leading to a deafening silence. He had so many questions, but he wasn't sure he wanted answers.

Three days. Liam had three days to figure it all out. What happened to his old life? His parents? Sarah?

The car announced they'd be there in ten minutes, and the older man spoke up: "My name's Liam. You named me Liam after the person you loved most—yourself. Just call me Lee."

Dismayed and speechless, Liam remained quiet for the rest of the journey, endlessly repeating the thought of only having three days left in his head.

Chapter 3

A sliver of light like a blade cut the air, revealing a square of beige hallway. A fluorescent strip light hummed. His movement woke the car from its energy saving stand-by mode. The door opened, revealing a small, enclosed parking garage. It was beige, the light was beige, the floor was beige. The gray pillars were off-white and had "Concourse A" scribbled on them. He climbed out of the car and twisted around to take in a view of the underground highway. He turned to the left, and across from him and to his left were more parking garages. These garages consisted of giant black boxes with parking spots, each one painted the same drywall beige as the wall, pillars, and floor. What was behind them, he did not know, and in fact, probably didn't want to know.

"We've arrived," the car's AI announced.

He stepped out and twisted around to take in a view of the underground highway. Across from him and to his left were more parking garages—there seemed to be many ways of getting down there. It was contrary to what he'd envisioned for the future; instead of taking off into the skies, people had dug deep beneath the ground.

"Let's go," Lee said and guided Liam to an elevator with a neon holographic sign that read "Athanasia Estates." As the doors parted open, he found himself standing in a traditional living room. On the left side was a wooden door with a peephole and no wall stretching back behind it. To the right was another room with just a frame—perhaps, it was the dining area or kitchen. The living room filled an entire wall, complete with a couch, fireplace, and chandeliers. A long hallway ran across the right side, ending in three bedrooms.

"They tried to make it as close to your memories as possible, so don't be too surprised," Lee said, but was cut off by a little voice from around the corner exclaiming, "SURPRISE!". A young girl, probably about eight years old, emerged wearing pajamas shaped like a teddy bear. Black hair and hazel eyes peeked out at Liam.

"Gramps?!" the little girl exclaimed, doing a full circle around him.

A man came running from the corner and scolding her. "Duchess! What did I say about being gentle with grandpa? He's in an unstable condition right now." The man standing slightly taller than Lee looked into Liam's eyes. He seemed to be of Asian-American descent: long black hair, dark-as-night eyes, friendly grin that seemed reassuring.

"Sorry again, nice meeting you—or seeing you again. Do you remember me?" said Andrew.

"Stop it, already! I already told you that he doesn't remember anyone," Lee said, exasperated.

"Not at all? Not even about us? Oh, my gosh! You have to come out to him again?! That's so funny! The only person I know that needs to come out twice to the same parent."

"Shut up, Andrew. This is not a laughing matter."

"Oh, please, we could all use some humor," Andrew replied with a smirk.

"Dad, what does coming out mean?" Duchess asked Andrew.

"My oh my, sweetheart," Andrew bent down and placed both hands on her shoulders. "Back when your Dad and I were young, folks felt they needed to... well... explain their love for someone of the same gender."

"That's strange!" she replied skeptically. "You should just love who you love."

"Yes, indeed, darling. It was definitely a peculiar time," Andrew smiled fondly. "So, then, Liam, this tiny one here is Duchess—your granddaughter. Your grandson should be around here somewhere..."

Son? My son is gay? Granddaughter? I think they said grandson, too. Liam felt like his head was spinning with all this new information. Up until now, these possibilities had never crossed his mind. He realized everyone was looking at him, waiting for him to respond.

"Duchess? That's her name?" Liam asked.

"Yep. 07-D-u-t-c-h-e-s-s-07. That's my tag," Duchess replied proudly. "Pretty clever name, right, grandpa?"

"Tag? What's that?" Liam questioned.

Duchess frowned and pouted unhappily at Liam's reaction.

Andrew then stepped in to explain: "Parents don't give children first names anymore; they use surnames until the child is old enough to choose their own. It's used universally for identification, a bit like your social security number was back in the day, combined with social media usernames."

"Well, that's dumb," Liam thought. Then, he remembered when his father called him dumb for his Instagram account tag.

Lee cut in, taking off his San Diego sweater to reveal a SF Giants baseball shirt: "Not everybody likes the names they were given." Liam knew it was a jab at him, but he couldn't help but take it in.

"Why don't we start dinner?" Andrew suggested, easing the tension between Liam and Lee. "Duchess, why don't you show Grand-Liam to the bedroom down the hall and go find your brother. Lee, help me out in the kitchen."

Andrew and Lee strolled down to the kitchen, with Andrew asking about the drive.

"Just don't," Lee muttered in response.

As they kept walking, Liam noticed Duchess watching him as if he was a stranger. Without warning, her mood shifted.

"Ok! Let's go," she said. "Your room is the last door on the left. Not much to entertain you, though. No games or anything."

"So, Duchess," Liam began. "Why that name?"

"My dads always called me a princess," she replied while they continued their journey down the hall. "But you always said I was more of a Duchess. Then you went away, and I didn't see you for a while. It made me sad, so I chose the name Duchess and added seven–to represent all the people I love in my life." Liam realized why she had been so excited to tell him her name. She put her hand on the door handle but stopped before opening it. "I'm glad you got a new body and are back," she ruminated with nostalgia. "I remember when grandpa Stevey got too old and went away; I'd miss you too if you did the same thing." She paused and then moved forward again, pushing open the door. "Anyways, here's your room."

Liam was taken aback by her sudden change of moods that could take him on a wild ride, then leave him without warning.

The door opened with the usual creak. He was slightly let down to discover it opened the same way as any other door. Inside was a white room with whitewashed walls and ceiling, a small closet to the left, and a window in front big enough to fit a queen-size bed and wooden dresser. A thin boy with pale, brunette hair lay on his back on the bed, arms behind his head and his right leg crossed over his left. He appeared to be Liam's age.

"Hey, Gramps is back!" Duchess exclaimed.

"You gotta be kidding me! Really? Oh, wow. Alright, I better go…" Boi said as he prepared to leave the room. "Wait, you think so? You're sure it'll work? Alright, then. Time to start a live feed. Hey, everyone, it's your boy Boi here, and I'm going to give you a glimpse into our future. May I introduce my 105-year-old grandpa, Liam." Boi hopped off the bed and moved towards his grandfather, eyes surveying him head to toe. Liam was dressed in black Sketchers sneakers, loose-fit jeans that sagged around his ankles, a plain white V-neck shirt accentuating his toned physique, and a no-frills black belt cinched tightly around his waist. His face bore blue eyes and a clean cut hairdo. "Wow, Gramps, did they really make you look this good? You remind me of retro times! Say hi to everybody," Boi said.

Liam was confused. There were only two people besides him in the room and no phones or cameras.

"Oh, shut, up. You act like your dumb friends are not the only ones who follow you. Hi, BayWarrior. Hi, Snake. Hi, KillerTim."

Duchess turned to Liam.

"He's talking to his friends at school. Don't worry about him. Nobody ever follows him. He's a loser, right, Loverboy?"

"That's all for now; check me out later," he quickly cut off the broadcast and glared at Duchess. "Don't call me that, brat. It's just Boi now."

"That's the name he chose, L-V-R-B-O-I-6-9, and everyone laughs at it. Even I think it's embarrassing, and I'm still a kid!" Duchess explained to Liam.

"This is so annoying! Dad won't pay for my application for a name change, and why do they let kids decide these things!"

"Boi, come set the table!" came a voice from another room.

"Ughhhhhh," Boi grumbled as he stormed away.

"How old is he?" Liam asked.

"Twenty," Duchess said, with a roll of her eyes. "My loser brother just hangs around inside talking to his friends and playing video games."

Liam spent the rest of his time inspecting his room while Duchess sat on her bed staring at him, then glancing idly up at the ceiling, kicking her legs back and forth, humming softly to herself.

"Right, so tell us about the thing you do. Staring Off. Is it like having a phone implanted in your head?"

Duchess shifted her gaze to Liam before replying. "What's a phone?"

"It was a device we used to communicate with each other, and to access information from the internet. It was like a tiny computer in our pockets."

"That doesn't make sense, but if you mean the chip, then yeah. They put this chip behind your ear, and then you use these contacts to see stuff or listen to music or... Wait! You don't even have it in?! So you're just... seeing things in real-time? How are you able to occupy yourself all this time?! Like without any tech?"

"So, you're seeing stuff in augmented reality, right?" asked Liam.

"Aug-what? I guess that makes sense, which explains why your name isn't hovering above your head. My friend CindyLoo was wondering the same thing, and CandyKiller wanted to know why you talked so much. Also, I told Boi and his friends to leave you alone," said Duchess.

Liam suddenly felt as though he was standing in a crowded room; he never liked being the center of attention, yet there he was like some kind of sideshow attraction.

"Dinner's ready."

Liam walked with Duchess across the living room and into the dining area, where Lee and Boi were already seated. The table was a brown wooden one and, above it, was a shining chandelier. Six chairs and six plates were set out for everybody.

Andrew emerged with a plate of pepperoni pizza. "No matter what year it is, you can't beat fresh-made pizza. Say what you want about that company, but they have certainly provided you with a great cooking setup."

He started to divide the slices of pizza among everyone; either it was really good or nobody wanted to say anything because it was so quiet. Lee kept his eyes downcast and Boi seemed lost in whatever device he had implanted in his head as he gazed off somewhere else in the room. Liam took a bite from his slice. Andrew noticed how weirded out Liam got.

"Hun, why don't your friends talk after they finish their dinner?"

"But—" Boi began to argue back, but then realized he was making Liam uneasy.

"Alright, then," he began to eat his piece of pizza but paused after a few bites to look over at the sixth seat next to Liam, which was empty and without a plate of food.

"So... What does this mean about your grandmother?"

Lee's face contorted in distress. "They said she's doing fine, but won't let me visit her. I don't trust that company. Dad, you would know, but you fucking..."

His shaking voice trailed off as he paused for a few moments to take a deep breath.

Andrew chimed in, "Hey, don't get too worked up about it; it won't do any good."

"No. You need to understand this—*I'm not apologizing* because you can't remember. At least then you might see what kind of person you were, what kind of person you have become, and the damage you've done to our family. You always put yourself first. And now I can't even see my dying mother one last time. This is your choice.

"What? I'm so confused. I'm really sorry, I never meant—" said Liam

"Dad—" Duchess said with a whimper.

"No! You did this yourself. Who are you to act like you don't even know us because of your memory loss? If only you would remember us, you'd understand what you've done all these years. Or maybe you wouldn't. You never really knew who we were before... You never knew me," Lee stood up abruptly and grabbed his plate. "You know what? I don't even think you know yourself anymore. It was all about work for you, wasn't it?"

Lee rushed away into the kitchen with his plate, and Andrew followed him with a concerned look on his face. The murmuring between the two men could barely be heard from the other room, but Duchess and Boi just kept eating.

Liam turned towards Duchess and Boi looking for an answer.

"Was I ever a bad father? When I was older?"

Boi answered first, "No... You were always nice to us, but you just weren't around very often. We only saw you on holidays like Thanksgiving and Christmas. Sometimes, we didn't get to see you at all because of your job."

"Yea, Daddy says you spend all this money to fix yourself when you could have been making us rich," Duchess added between bites of her pizza.

"Your relationship with dad wasn't that great when grandma got sick."

The thought of Sarah never left his mind, so he rarely considered the woman he had married. But what kind of person was she? Who would marry this flawed man?

"What was your grandmother like? Emily, right?"

Duchess and Boi shared a meaningful glance, conveying the immense love they felt for her in one silent moment. They were about to speak when Lee interrupted.

"Ok, kids. Let's go. We'll take the rest home. I think it's best to let Grandpa get some rest tonight."

Lee stepped out, fully dressed in his coat, followed by Andrew. It seemed as if Lee had won the argument.

"You're leaving?" Liam stood up from his chair in disbelief.

"Look, Dad, I'm sorry for causing a fuss. We took a train here and found a hotel at the last minute. We're all on edge. We need time to process this, too. Maybe a good night's sleep will help us all out."

Liam barely knew these people, but he didn't want to be alone; the fear of having to do this without them was paralyzing him. He searched for something to say that could convince them to stay—anything would do.

"I-I'm sorry. Please look, I don't know who I've become, but I'm sorry."

Andrew, Duchess, and LoverBoy had made their way over to the elevator and were putting on their coats.

Lee approached Liam.

"I don't know if you understand this, but the docs wanted me to make sure it sank in. You need to stay here for a week or else you'll lose your memories forever. It's important. Patrol officers are outside the house so you are secure, and we'll try to make it as comfortable as possible. We'll bring whatever you need," Lee paused before continuing. "Liam, I'm sure you can make it through this situation. I know how strong you are."

Lee walked to the elevator and Liam was left standing by himself in a living room that suddenly felt very empty. He headed to the kitchen looking for a drink to settle his nerves, but of course there wasn't any alcohol there. Hardly five minutes after everyone left, he heard a disturbance from outside. He went to the lounge window and peeked out.

He hadn't braved the outdoors yet. When he glanced out the window, he was astounded by the forest that lay before him. He couldn't believe this was the same space he knew as a park earlier; it had been transformed into an oasis of towering redwoods, a mini-forest across from Muir Woods. A dusty pathway snaked its way to the entrance, wide enough for joggers or bikers to traverse. His cottage wasn't alone there, though; another one sat nearby, and it seemed to come straight out of a fairytale. Lights were on inside and Liam heard muffled conversations and people moving around. Suddenly, a woman emerged from the front door. She looked to be his age or older, with long golden-brown hair down her back. She had on athletic gear—a workout sports bra paired with leggings— that flaunted her petite figure. She released her bun and let her hair blow in the breeze, each strand glimmering like diamonds in the sunlight. Taking a deep breath, she glared back at Liam and then turned left.

Liam hastily jerked back to conceal himself, and peered again, trying to see if she had noticed him. Her eyes stuck in his mind; they were a color of blue he had never seen before, so striking that it made him think for sure that the color was fake. Then, he noticed her hair, falling over one eye as she pushed it aside. She smiled radiantly at the nature around her. Noticing her small nose and larger-than-life lips, he moved on to study the rest of her attire, which enhanced her figure in a way that seemed intentional yet subtle. He found his gaze lingering unnaturally long on her legs. Was this a trend in this future? He wondered what brand her white running shoes were.

As Liam looked closer, he saw the words "Athanasia". Ugh. He looked away and back again. Athanasia. The clothing she was wearing was all branded with the same logo. Two men then came out of the house; Liam noticed they were dressed in militant uniforms, all white, and had the same logo on their clothes. As Liam suspected, they must have been guards—no matter what hour, place or day you go, if people are matching and have the same logo, they carry a weapon with them. She started giving out orders while pointing at something and quickly went back inside with the two men following close behind. He remembered Lee talking about sending someone to watch him.

This could be a perfect opportunity to demand answers, Liam thought. He put on his serious face and psyched himself up before heading towards the door. When he had taken two steps forward, a hand stopped him across his chest.

A man dressed like one of the guards was standing before Liam.

"Greetings, Liam. I'm Tyler, and I'll be watching your place tonight. If you need anything, I'll be here all night long."

"I just wanted to talk to that lady—I need answers!"

"You will get them tomorrow, but it seems like you need some rest first. I understand the situation is tough, but that's what I was told to do by my superiors. You can accept it or not, but either way, you must rest."

The guard kept his arm across Liam's chest as if he expected him to run away. Liam had a split-second where he considered doing so, but when he looked into the guard's eyes, he could see something saying "Don't". So, Liam walked back inside and closed the door behind him.

Sinking down against the door, he hugged his knees close to his chest and felt his heart thumping against his legs. Everything hit him at once; he'd never felt so confined and helpless in his life. Yesterday had been the best day of his life, and now? He wanted his mom. He craved the family he'd lost; the youngest among his cousins with no siblings left to rely on. The strangers surrounding him were telling him things he would never follow through with. His memories of Sarah were becoming fuzzy, too—he had no photos or phones with her image anymore. She only existed in his mind.

He got up, headed to the entranceway, and opened the door.

"Tyler, right?"

"Yes. How can I help you?"

"Do you have a pen? Paper's not necessary."

"Here you go."

"Thanks."

Liam snatched up the pen and closed the door behind him. He began walking back into the living room, and stopped for a moment, glancing into the dining area at the knife that Lee had used to slice the pizza earlier. Perhaps he should just end it all—Sarah and his parents weren't around anymore, why hang on any longer? Seemingly, no one would care if he vanished from existence, either. Liam slowly paced into the dining area, then picked up the knife with his left hand and placed it flat in his right hand; he could feel the cold steel press against his skin. The thought of giving up was so strong now. But then it went away; why had he even considered such a thing?

Sprinting towards his bedroom, Liam grabbed a marker and started drawing on the far wall above the bed. When finished, he stepped back to admire what he'd made: it was an artful representation of Sarah Smith with her name written beneath it—a reminder of when she had said "yes". "Never forget" he wrote underneath.

Huddled up on the bed, he faced the wall, feeling estranged from his family and the world. He didn't know why this had happened to him, but he was determined to uncover what had become of Sarah. That meant escaping from there as soon as possible.

Meanwhile, the woman who had been seen outside was just finishing her shower and donning a robe with "bliss" written across it. As she leaned towards the mirror, two clear contacts were inserted into her eyes that suddenly opened a world of new possibilities: artwork materialized on the walls and the lighting brightened, while a drop-down menu with an oldies playlist played in one corner of her vision. Suddenly, Dr. Tithonus' face appeared out of nowhere and asked how she was holding up.

"I just got my first workout in," she replied. "Physically, I'm feeling great."

"Have you gone over to check on Liam, yet?" inquired Dr. Tithonus.

"No," said Bliss. "I ordered everybody else to let him have time to process everything—he can be rather impulsive." At this point, Bliss became suspicious. "Is there something you're not telling me?"

"Everything is under control." Dr. Tithonus declared confidently.

"Don't lie to me," Bliss replied impatiently.

"Alright, I can admit that something worrying has arisen. But it's better if you don't know what it is, yet," he explained.

"What could be so concerning that it frightens even you?" she asked with apprehension in her voice.

"I'll tell you when I'm certain of everything. Just make sure Liam stays where he is for now. I need to go."

And with that, Dr. Tithonus disappeared, leaving Bliss alone in the bathroom. She walked out of the bathroom and into the living room, which was full of virtual ads and art popping up around her, as well as a virtual fireplace providing warmth and comfort. She looked out the window at the cottage where Liam was residing and felt an overwhelming sense of uneasiness.

Chapter 4

The birds were singing their morning songs. Liam's eyes fluttered open. He felt a momentary confusion, thinking he had woken up in his old room, until a drawing of Sarah on the wall caught his eye. He had stayed asleep longer than he planned, after the exhaustion from the day before had caught up with him. He got out of bed and examined the drawing of Sarah, wondering what could have happened that she wasn't part of his life anymore. Did they betray each other? Or did something occur while he was unconscious.

He decided to erase this thought and focus on figuring out what to do next. He headed to the kitchen to get some cleaning supplies and grabbed a rag from one of the drawers and stain removers from underneath the sink before passing by the dining room table. He stopped suddenly; something was off. A second glance at the table confirmed it: the knife he had picked up the night before during a moment of weakness was missing. His mind raced as fear threatened to creep onto his face—someone had been inside his house while he was sleeping! He quickly rushed to the front door and opened it.

"Good morning, Liam! I hope you slept well," Tyler was still there, outside.

"Morning. You were here all night? Outside?" asked Liam.

"Yes, sir. Gets pretty cold if I must say so," said Tyler.

"Did anyone come inside last night?" Liam attempted to sound nonchalant.

"Nope. We wanted you to have your privacy."

"Ok, just checking," replied Liam as he closed the door, then walked back to the leather couch in the living room. He'd seen enough movies to realize this had become a prison of sorts. But why would they lie about the guard coming inside? Maybe there wasn't one, or maybe his mind was playing tricks on him. Liam got up and headed toward the door, wondering what he should do next, when suddenly, someone knocked on it three times. He opened the front door to see Tyler again.

"Liam, Bliss is ready to see you now. She's waiting at the other house." *Crap. Already?* thought Liam. However, he figured that might be an opportunity for more answers, and decided to at least go meet Bliss.

As he wandered down the path connecting the cottages, Liam recalled the mysterious woman, Bliss, whom he had seen. He picked up his pace, shaking off any lingering doubts about evil corporations and malevolent villains. He reminisced about the embarrassment of acting like a jerk in front of his family when they had all come to visit.

Before he knew it, he arrived at the entrance to the house. The idea of peeking through the window crossed his mind, but he resisted. Tyler's voice echoed from afar, urging him not to be a creep and just go inside. Liam took a breath and tapped on the door before pushing it open. As soon as he stepped inside, everything looked familiar: same living room layout, same decorations, yet no one in sight. A melody suddenly floated out from the kitchen, which caught Liam's attention straight away; it was none other than the "Galway Girl" song! He remembered how, back in college, he and his friends would belt that tune during St. Paddy's Day celebrations. *And I ask you friend, what's a fella to do? Because her hair was black and her eyes were blue...*

A cheer came from the kitchen. His heart warmed with nostalgia, and a smile crept across his face. He strolled towards the room, where the same woman he'd seen the day before was dancing and cutting food at the dining table, completely unaware of his presence.

"Ahem," Liam said.

At the sound of his voice, it seemed like time froze, and she jumped slightly in surprise. "Hi," she said cheerfully.

"Um... You wanted to see me?" Liam asked.

The woman whirled around and grabbed something from behind her, revealing a delicious BLT sandwich. She brought it to him with a smile on her face and told him to have a seat. Apparently, this was all for him to make him feel more comfortable, which seemed odd since they had just met. Confused, Liam inspected the sandwich and questioned what was going on. He noticed that this was his favorite type of sandwich—how did she know?

"What is this? I mean all of this, the song, the sandwich, the old-school house, the guards. Why am I the only one who doesn't know anything?"

"Okay, wow, too much? No hello? Alright, then, let's start with introductions. My name is Bliss. I'm here to help you get your memories back, just like everyone else."

"Is that what this was all about? Like, what the fuck?" said Liam

"I apologize, I was trying to do things you would like," said Bliss.

"That's what I'm saying! How do you even know what I like?!" shouted Liam.

"Please, settle down, we just want the best for you."

"That is what I mean! Who is 'we'?"

Liam began to question if she was doing it on purpose or not; yet, it seemed like she was genuinely distressed and sorry.

"Look, I didn't mean to yell. Yesterday, I was proposing to my girlfriend in Tahoe. Next thing I know, I am here," Liam said, trying to calm himself down.

"Oh, wow. That was your last memory? Proposing to Sarah?" asked Bliss

"Yeah. Wait... you know her?" asked Liam with surprise.

"No, I'm sorry, but indeed I've heard of her. It must be an overwhelming feeling knowing that is the last memory you have in that world before entering this one."

Liam sadly looked away and nodded his head in agreement.

"I can't understand how hard it must be—memories are so important to us all. When I met the love of my life, he came out of nowhere. I was too busy building my career and pursuing my dreams to think about relationships. We happened to be interns at the same job and almost immediately connected; it felt like destiny. He made everyday tasks enjoyable and always supported me, no matter how much our interests clashed. He was my best friend and for the first time ever, there was someone who constantly stayed in my mind through good or bad," Bliss let out a nostalgic sigh as she concluded her story. "Tell me about her," she said abruptly, quickly changing the subject.

"What do you mean?" asked Liam, confused.

"Just your last days with Sarah. I'm interested in hearing about them from your perspective."

"Alright. Well—"

Liam talked. Talking helped him ease his mind. He discussed things that he'd forgotten for a while; conversations he had with his parents, as well as memories leading up to his final moments with Sarah. She would chuckle at his dad's awkward moments and make this adorable expression when he spoke about his mom. Though she worked for the evil corporation and had ulterior motives, it was nice talking to Bliss; he finally felt like he could breathe again. He felt secure, though he eventually realized what she had planned.

"I don't suppose I can leave, can I?" Liam murmured quietly.

Her smile faded as she shook her head no.

"What would happen if I tried?" Liam questioned calmly.

"To tell you the truth, I don't know," she replied gravely. "Legally speaking, you're a threat to our company. This technology is groundbreaking; Dr. Tithonus and this company believe that they've found the key to immortality.

"Can you imagine anything more groundbreaking than that?" she continued on without waiting for an answer. "But you're now someone who poses a danger to the company's interests. It would alarm shareholders if they learned that our technology wasn't yet viable for human testing.

"The board members are powerful people," she added ominously. "Like any other corporation, we need funds, and developing this technology costs quite a bit of money; perhaps, more than just money alone." She hesitated before continuing, then said softly, "And creating human vessels? The technology necessary to save the human brain? You have no idea what you've given up."

"What have I sacrificed?" Liam asked, confused. "I wish I could comprehend that. Have you ever fallen so deeply in love with someone that you'd give up anything, including this 'immortality', just to spend the rest of your life with them? Our problems are nothing alike."

"That's not necessarily true. Getting your memories back should tell you what happened to Sarah and everything else," Bliss said.

Suddenly, there was a knock on the door.

"Grandpa? Are you here? That weirdly polite stranger out front directed me here," a voice came from outside.

Bliss opened the door to reveal Boi standing there.

"Hey, I'm here to take my grandfather to Dr. Tithonus' office downtown," he said.

"Of course, come in," Bliss replied.

Boi walked in and saw Liam.

"Where's your dad or the rest of the family?" Liam asked him.

"Oh, they couldn't make it. They sent me instead," Boi answered half-heartedly as his gaze strayed away, almost like he was messaging someone.

Liam got up and headed for the door; he glanced at Bliss, who stood in the doorway with a smile on her face.

"Well, thanks for speaking with me," Liam said uncertainly, not sure if that were true or not.

"We can talk more when you come back again," she smiled wider. "Maybe, I'll show you around this new city."

"I'd like that," he wasn't sure why he'd said that either, but couldn't really deny it now even if he wanted to.

"Can we use your elevator?" Boi asked her.

"Of course," she nodded her head.

The two made their way to the elevator and rode it down together silently until Boi finally spoke up.

"Who was that?" asked Boi

"I have no idea; she works for Dr. Tithonus," Liam responded cautiously.

"She seemed kind of familiar," Boi added innocently enough, but Liam still felt almost guilty in response, thinking Boi had noticed more than he let on before continuing on to say, "Do you mind if I do a live stream while we're here? My followers have increased since your story leaked to the media, and everyone is interested now."

"Sure, I don't care," said Liam

"What's up, everyone? It's your boy here, giving you all an update. Today's adventure? I'm taking Grandpa to the doctor. What secrets will be revealed? Stay tuned. Please share with friends and subscribe to me if you're interested! Could we be the last generation to not die?!"

Liam raised an eyebrow. "Is this some kind of school project?"

"No. It's interesting, and people are starting to take notice," Boi replied.

"Ah, popularity. You want to be popular," said Liam knowingly.

"Oh, please! I don't care what people think. This is my chance to document history—maybe even start a career as a film director," Boi responded eagerly as a black town car pulled up for them to get in.

As he continued filming, Boi asked for the address, but was quickly informed by the car that it had been programmed in already. He laughed nervously and decided to explain, "Yeah, everyone connected these days—you can pretty much look up anyone or anything."

Liam queried curiously, "Really? Could you look up an old friend of mine then? Sarah?"

Boi seemed taken aback by the request and replied hesitantly, "Uhh, why would I... Well, ok, if my friends seem to want me to, but who do you have in mind? You'll have to be more specific; there are thousands of Sarahs out there!"

He admitted sheepishly, "Last name is Smith. Her middle name is Marie; she was born in New York City and moved to SF at age of twenty-one. She has blonde hair and hazel eyes, always smiling. She's outdoorsy, and she'd be my age now... Or she could very well be dead from old age."

"Well, if it's this woman you're talking about, she is alive. About 106 years old, I'd assume? Lives in a city up north called Forestville. Let me dive deeper and find out what she used to look like.

"Wait, can you pull up a photo from a particular date?" Liam asked.

'Yeah, man. You might look young, but you sure sound like a grandpa!" Boi joked.

"Check any photos from June 10th, 2024—I may still be in it," Liam suggested.

"Hmm... Nope, no photos of you here," replied Boi.

Liam's heart sank.

"On those dates, it's just some pictures of her hiking in... Tahoe, most likely. It stinks that you don't have the chip inserted. I would just show you how to do this," whimpered Boi.

"Tahoe?! That must be Sarah—we have to go to where she is!" Liam jumped onto Boi and gave him a hug of excitement. "That must be her! Forestville—we need to get going!"

"What? No way! You'll get me into so much trouble!" Boi protested.

"Please—this was someone very special to me, I loved her," pleaded Liam.

"What? No way! You love Grandma—you ended up with Grandma! You can't love anyone else!" Boi exclaimed angrily.

"Look, I'm sorry—I don't even know your grandmother or you for that matter. I'm lost, and this person is the only one who knows me more than anyone else in the world; we once loved each other deeply!" Liam tried to appeal to Boi's emotions as he continued speaking. "You named yourself LoverBoi, right? That must have been for some girl—have you ever felt as though something is missing without them? The sweetest dreams of them never being as good as the real thing?" Liam worked on manipulating his way into getting Boi on his side. "Plus, it'll make for an amazing documentary—all these people watching want to see a great love story come true, don't they?"

"Grandpa, I don't..." Boi's eyes unfocused and looked ahead. "What? My-My followers exploded. Wow, I've never had this many," Boi started to become popular on his live feed.

"See? People agree. Everyone loves a love story," Liam said.

"What do you all think? Ugh, okay. But *after* the appointment. We can still make it back by tonight," Boi gave in.

"I apologize, Boi. I'm sure your grandma is a great person, but I don't know her. The last thing I remember was proposing to Sarah, she said yes, and then... Here I am."

"Darn. That must be tough," Boi sympathized.

"You bet it is! This is all strange to me... Not what I expected my life was going to be like with all that you and your dad have mentioned so far. Like, what was I doing for work?" Liam asked.

"You were a scientist," Boi answered simply.

"No way, I never went to school for science, there's no way I'm that smart," Liam explained.

"What did you envision your life would be like?" Boi inquired.

"I'd marry Sarah and move back east to New York, where I'd work as a sports writer; we both wanted to find a small town to call home. She loved the idea of living in a small town more than anything," Liam remembered.

"I had no idea that about that. I thought you were a traveler, not the kind of person who would settle down in one place! I saw pictures of you with Grandma—you both never looked really content in one place. Even when work became a full-time thing for you, your joy seemed never-ending. I never guessed sports writer could have been an alternative career for you. I just assumed you were a nerd growing up," Boi said incredulously.

"What do you mean? I love going to games and playing sports!" Liam replied, confused.

"Nope. You were into science. Wait, that means... Did they not tell you? You worked at Athanasia—can't remember what title you had, but it sounded like it was pretty high up there."

"No way! In school, I barely scraped by my anatomy class," Liam said in disbelief.

"Well, what can I say? Your grandmother was employed by them, too," Boi responded.

Liam's insides twisted in his stomach as he realized his missing memories could not be an accident. It was impossible to find out everything he needed to know and track Sarah down within two days, but luckily, she hadn't ventured far away, so it was feasible. He'd just need to get the answers from Dr. Tithonus first, then he'd be on his way to her.

"Are you getting more followers now?" Liam asked Boi, his tone tinged with curiosity.

Boi's eyes unglazed as he replied, "Yeah. A lot. But... I stopped recording."

Liam's eyebrows lifted in surprise. "What? Why?"

"I am not allowed to record in the office. And Grandpa..." Boi stumbled on his words before correcting himself, "I mean, Liam. I want to help you. You are right. I chose LoverBoy because of a girl that I really like; we've known each other since second grade. She always used to call me lover boy 'cause she thought I was a catch and could get any girl. But secretly, I wanted her. I figured if I started streaming, maybe she would watch it and notice me," Boi paused for a moment before continuing. "But besides that, hanging out with you has been pretty cool, too. Learning things about you and seeing all these similarities between us has been interesting. I'd like to learn more and see where this goes."

A small smile appeared on Liam's face as he replied, "Thank you. You know, I don't know how great of a father I was back then, but Lee must have been a good one. 'Cause you seem like a great kid."

Boi laughed for a moment before saying, "You calling me a kid feels weird, though, since we're around the same age."

"Yeah, it does feel weird," Liam agreed.

"From now on," Boi said, "you can call me Steven. That's the name I wanted to change my name to."

Liam raised an eyebrow in confusion before asking, "Why not just start calling yourself that now?"

"Well," Boi explained, "until we pay and fill out an application, my displayed name will still be LoverBoy. The display name is the only name people will call you, so you have to be careful."

The two men laughed, their relationship growing stronger by the moment.

Liam paused and asked, "Do you remember your great-grandparents?"

"No. They were gone before I was born," Steven stated.

"Coincidentally, my father's name was Steven, so maybe I can tell you stories about them. You look so much like him," Liam said fondly.

"I would love to hear those stories," Steven responded.

The car pulled up to the Athanasia building and Liam stepped out, owning a newfound admiration for Steven. His gaze shifted to the towering skyscraper in front of him; the secrets it held had been kept hidden for so long, and that day he'd finally get some answers.

Chapter 5

Steven and Liam waited outside the entrance elevator.

"Ready for this, Liam?" newly named Steven asked.

"I haven't been ready since I woke up, but it's now or never," replied Liam. The elevator doors opened and Dr. Tithonus stepped out, smiling at them.

"Hello again, Liam," the Doctor said before turning to Steven. "Ah, and you must be his grandson... LoverBoi?"

"It's Steven," Liam corrected as he smiled warmly at his grandson.

"Ah, Steven! Pleased to meet you. Well, thanks for coming. This way." They followed the Doctor into the elevator, and it started to move upwards. "This shouldn't take all day. We first want to check on you, make sure nothing is going wrong with your body before we attempt to fix your memories and download the rest of them to you in a few hours—nearly all of which will be spent waiting around."

They arrived at the floor of Athenasia and stepped out, following the doctor's lead.

"So, how are you going to download my memories back into me?" asked Liam curiously

"Follow me this way, and I'll explain," replied the Dr., continuing, "the procedure is quite simple: we just download the information to the chip inside your brain—the same type that everyone has that allows them to augment reality, a process done by computers—and once it downloads, that chip transfers the data over time to your brain until all the data becomes a permanent part of your natural stream of consciousness."

As they strolled along the hallway, Liam noticed that the office looked like a normal doctor's office—there was a receptionist at the front desk, and multiple doors lining either side of the corridor. The only difference was the lack of patients—all Liam could see were workers. Every time he walked past them, they would all stare at him as if he were their only customer. It wasn't until Dr. Tithonus opened one of the doors that Liam remembered this room—where he first woke up.

"Remember this?" he asked, and a sinister smirk appearing on his face. "Steven, you can stay here too. A nurse will be in soon to check on you both. Do you need anything?" The two shook their heads before the doctor left with a warm smile and closed the door behind him.

The atmosphere felt heavy in the room as Steven began pacing around, examining things that had been augmented during Liam's stay. Eventually, he made his way over to the rolling chair and sat down, facing Liam.

"So, tell me about yourself," Steven started off by asking.

"What do you want to know?" inquired Liam eagerly.

"Let us begin with where you grew up? What was life like there? Your hobbies? Anything else that comes to mind!" Steven suggested.

Liam began to explain: "I was born in San Francisco in 2000. I was your typical kid growing up then; I played sports and loved reading comic books, DC over Marvel any day!"

"I didn't know that about you. Wait. DC? They went extinct. They sucked. Marvel was way better," said Steven, still not entirely focused.

"What? DC is way better. No way Batman could go extinct," Liam exclaimed.

"Yeah. Disney purchased the rights and assimilated them into Marvel. All the main characters were under one big company. So you were kind of a nerd, right? Did Sarah share your interests? Comics or sports, maybe?" asked Steven

"Uh... no. She was more into reality TV and famous people. Disdained sports, so when I wanted to attend matches, I had my buddies, and she had her pals," said Liam

"Huh," Steven said, smirking away.

"What?" asked Liam

"I never knew you were passionate about sports, but Grandma definitely was; she used to take us with her to games all the time. Bet you that she was also interested in comic books as well."

"No, you don't understand. You don't have to share activities or thoughts to be in love. People can have different interests," snapped Liam

"I'm not trying to say otherwise, but you haven't really explained why you love Sarah yet," said Steven.

"Geez. I feel like I'm being interviewed or something. Alright, alright. Alright," Liam cringed and heaved a big sigh. "I was 21 years old at the time. Living in San Francisco's Marina District, and I used to jog across the Golden Gate Bridge early in the morning. One day, it was very thick and foggy; you could hardly make out anything. I have this habit of peering at tourists as I run past them; that day, my eyes locked with a blonde woman's eyes; she had been admiring the view from the bridge despite its poor visibility. But then, disaster struck—I slipped and fell right in front of her! She was the only one around who noticed—kind-hearted soul that she was, she ran over to help me up, and we made our way to a café at the end of the bridge. She got me ice for my ankle injury, and we sat down together to chat. Turns out she had just moved there to work as a traveling nurse.

"We soon became really close friends after that; we enjoyed going hiking and spending evenings on fun dates together. That photo of Tahoe? That's where I proposed to her on June 10th, 2024. And that's the last memory I have with her..." he said, completing his story.

"Wow! You had a whole other life none of us knew about. I mean, if you stayed with Sarah, then I wouldn't be here. Crazy! But still, tell me about what she was like?" Steven continued.

Liam almost seemed offended by the question, but he answered regardless. "I don't remember much about her. All I know is that when I talk about her, it always seems different. You just get this feeling that she was something special to me... like a goddess or something."

Liam looked off into the distance and sighed; he wished more than anything to recover his lost memories.

Steven smiled in an attempt to reassure him, "Don't worry, we'll get them back soon enough." Liam forced himself to smile back, trying to imagine what it would be like to have an actual brother.

Out of the blue, the door opened, and a young nurse walked through wearing a face mask that covered half her face. "Alright, Dr. Long. You look good; your heart rate is a bit elevated, but that's probably just your nerves."

"Wait, you didn't do anything to me yet," said Liam confused.

"Oh, the room scans us once we walk in. Something to do with the high-tech cameras," explained Steven.

"So, Liam, the next step is some questions to see if your memory has improved, and then we'll go downstairs to get you ready for tomorrow's procedure. First question: have you remembered anything since yesterday?" asked the nurse.

"In fact, he knows he used to work here," said Steven, interjecting.

"Oh, that's great! You remember working here?" asked the nurse.

"I guess... Yes," said Liam.

"He just hasn't had enough water to drink; can you grab some? Right, Grandpa?" Steven nudged him playfully.

"Yeah, that would be lovely," Liam replied.

"Right away, Doctor Long. I'll be back soon." The nurse smiled with her eyes and walked away.

"What was that?" asked Liam.

"Didn't you see that? She called you Doctor Long and was super formal with you! I bet there were a lot of people here who looked up to you as their superior," said Steven.

"Okay... What are you getting at?" asked Liam.

"I bet you have access to a lot of things around here, like information. She said the machine is downstairs," Steven explained.

"But she's coming back and there are probably cameras," Liam pointed out.

"You wanted to fight the world a second ago. Answers are right here, why wait?" Steven challenged.

"Shit... okay... You're right," Liam conceded.

Liam and Steven stepped out into the hallway. Was all that noise they heard coming from before just a show? Making their way towards the elevator, they heard voices and decided to take the emergency exit stairs leading to the lower floor instead.

The two walked out of the stairwell and saw the same type of hall as on the previous floor. They each chose different sides of the hallway, Liam taking left, Steven taking right.

The first door Steven tried was a closet filled with boxes; Liam's first try led him to a waiting area like the one he'd woken up in upstairs. After checking out Steven's next door—which appeared to be some kind of office—they searched through drawers, scanned the computer for answers, yet came up empty-handed. The pair continued onwards; Liam went for his next door and called Steven over: "Check this out!"

Steven and Liam made their way to the smaller room. To the right stood a lounge area and just beyond it, a computer setup with recording equipment staring out from behind an immense glass window. Wires snaked away from this station to another door across the far side of the room. Peering through the glass, Steven spotted a huge two-story space filled with towering six-foot servers on one side. Adjacent to them were two operating tables in the room's center.

"Should we go in?" Steven asked.

"Why not? That direction takes us closer to answers," Liam replied.

"Do you want me to record this?"

"No, let's not take any chances; who knows who might see your live feed?"

The pair descended the steel stairs into the server room. Steven strolled around examining the servers while Liam studied the table with wires connected to the servers in order to provide power to a head that would lie there.

"How is it accessed?" Steven inquired.

"I don't know for sure. But look here—another door!"

In the back of the room was a heavy steel door. It took them some effort to open it, but they eventually managed. The long corridor past the entryway contained twelve doors on either side, each with its own name. They stepped into the first room on the left, marked "Elon Bezos," grandson of Amazon's founder. Inside, there was a single computer beside a colossal test tube filled with an adult-sized amniotic sac.

"Whose body is that?" Steven asked as he moved closer to the computer. Its monitor displayed a biography of the person in the container. "Looks like they're replicating human reproduction through gene splicing according to their preferences. We've entered a sci-fi movie now! You can even craft yourself an exact replica or upgrade your former self with whatever you'd like—blue eyes, for example. It's all just code."

"Is there any information about me or Dr. Tithonus?" Liam posed the question aloud.

"Not here, at least not on this computer. Let's check out what's behind one of the other doors," Steven suggested as they walked down the hallway, and he noticed that each door was labeled with the name of someone influential or wealthy. "Seems like they're doing people with power first," he realized aloud.

"Well, they must have gotten funding from some source—or rather, how I got mine," Liam remarked thoughtfully.

As Steven and Liam walked down the hallway, Steven noticed every name was of someone in power or rich.

At the end of the hallway, they stopped in front of the last four doors.

"Let's check these," Steven said. He opened the first door, but no name was listed; it seemed to be a storage room. The next door had a plaque with the name "Dr. Tithonus" inscribed on it. Inside was a computer and various diagnostic equipment typical of someone doing research or tests.

The third door bore Emily Long's full name: Emily Michela Long, MD. Inside, was a secure computer surrounded by numerous medical tools and an operating seat in the middle of the room. *That must have been her workstation for performing surgeries and monitoring patients' vital signs remotely*, Liam thought.

The fourth and final door revealed Liam's name: Liam Van Long III, CEO & Founder of Blue Corp Industries Incorporated. On the wall beside his desk were several monitors displaying live feeds from facilities across the world and financial reports on companies that he had invested in. There was also a small workbench with various devices and tools used for robotics engineering projects.

The two men looked at each other in amazement as they realized what they had stumbled upon—a hidden laboratory where powerful individuals were being cloned or enhanced through genetic modification—all done under one roof! Steven began to feel uneasy as he thought about how much power that place held, while Liam recalled his past experiences with advanced technology and how it could be abused if not managed properly. He knew that he would have to find some way to keep this secret from getting out into public knowledge—this was something that could unravel entire nations if it fell into the wrong hands!

"What do we check first?" Steven asked.

"Let's start with the most obvious," Liam replied.

They entered Liam's room and saw an empty skeleton of a space. Computer parts were strewn all over the floor, and tracks from something large led out the door where the body sac had been. Liam frowned in frustration. Steven reminded him there were still two more rooms to search through, but Liam was only interested in Dr Tithonus' room. With no agreement formed, they split up.

As soon as he stepped into Dr Tithonus' room, Liam knew this was the place that held answers. Multiple sacs of growing bodies lined one wall; some in the early stages of development, while others seemed almost ready to be used at any moment. Each tube described different characteristics of its inhabitant. Liam searched for a computer, but it wouldn't turn on; it was merely a blank screen. He started to look through drawers and spotted a pair of glasses in the top right one, prompting him to reconsider his choice not to take them. Upon putting them on, the paintings lit up around him and the lights brightened in contrast. The tubes showed more detailed information about what was being grown inside them; these weren't just for research purposes—it looked like someone had ordered special bodies. As if on cue, the computer activated and became visible due to augmented reality.

At first, he flailed his arms like a toddler trying to reach something out of grasp. Then, he began prodding the desktop items, as if his grandfather was teaching him how to use a computer. There were many folders of information that he needed to look at, but he didn't know how to save them or download them for later. Any folder that mentioned his family or himself was at the top of his priority list. He eventually came across a file with his name on it, but it had a password requirement that was preventing him from opening it. After much thought, he had an idea: he used Google to search for the name of the doctor in charge of this project, and what he found was an old Greek tale about a man who wished for immortality. The god granted his wish—but did not give him youth. The man kept getting older and older until life became so unbearable that death felt like a sweet relief. Tithonus is a Greek character from a poem? If this wasn't the doctor's real name, why would he choose it? He tried tithonus as a password. No luck. Remembering the ancient poem from 1859, he tried Eros1859, the title of the story. It worked! Inside the folder were videos, emails, Excel documents, and theories galore—so much that he didn't even know where to begin.

He clicked on the first video that appeared, which showed a procedure in the operating room. On the table was an elderly man, and next to him, a body bag. In it, he realized, was his own current body. The staff wheeled the gurney out and a glass dome rose up around the two bodies. The bubble quickly filled with a neon green fluid, and then servers outside of it began lighting up. Out from the back of the operating table came small robotic hands carrying wires, which were attached to both the servers and the table within the bubble. As Liam watched this process, he flicked through some other files until he saw an email labeled "Care to explain?"

Bliss had recently sent an email that read: *I thought you said this was an accident. What is going on? How could you do this?* Attached to the email was a video of Dr. Tithonus in the control center of the operating room with another person. It showed all the events leading up to the disastrous event that Liam had witnessed; Dr. Tithonus pacing back and forth, getting a coffee, spilling it, and then yelling at the other guy before running over to hit the abort button. The video showed how as he spilled the coffee, the servers started sparking, and when he hit the button, the bodies started shaking uncontrollably until it went dark. Liam replayed both videos, watching them until the end.

Liam trembled. His fears were justified. What had happened that led to this? He kept searching, finding a series of emails from someone calling themselves the Board Members. The emails had started out friendly enough when asking about the progress of the project, but they had become more insistent and threatening as time went on, apparently demanding stocks in the company from Liam and another guy called Albert. The last email from the board stated that since Liam's mind was not fully downloaded, he posed a risk and liability for future investors.

"What are you doing here? Where is Liam?" a voice boomed from another room.

No! thought Liam. He was so close to unlocking the mystery—he was sure there must be some basic way to download the files, but he didn't possess the knowledge needed. Now he frantically searched for old records, anything associated with Sarah or his family... But then, his computer froze up and wouldn't let him click on anything.

"Finally, you're here!" Bliss burst into the room with Steven lurking in the background behind her. He looked like he was trying to avoid being blamed for something.

"What's happening?" asked Liam.

"I know you're anxious right now, but I'm on your side," Bliss replied. "We need to get out of here before the guards arrive."

"Guards? Why are they coming for me?"

Bliss hesitated before answering. "It seems that restoring your memories is more complicated than we thought. The board members who paid for your procedure are debating what to do with you at this very moment. Some are saying they should keep trying, while others... They think of you and all of us as just property. They don't see you as human, Liam; understand that."

"Property? What are they going to do with me?"

"It depends on whether or not they can restore your memories. If they cannot, then it means losing a lot of money, and you will be seen as a failure, which could scare future investors. But if they decide that you are just property, then..." Bliss trailed off.

"Then what?"

"They'll try again with a new body and dispose of this defecting chip," said Bliss grimly.

"No, this can't be happening! I am me," cried Liam.

"Are you saying they want to kill my grandad?" Steven asked in shock.

"I didn't know. This isn't supposed to be the way. We were creating a world without suffering, where disease and death would no longer exist—we wanted to be immortal here on Earth. But right now, it doesn't matter—there's no time," Bliss said urgently before racing down the hall. Liam and Steven exchanged a nervous glance before they followed her.

"We need to go this way to the elevator," she called over her shoulder.

"Can't they see us on camera?" Steven asked, but Bliss shook her head.

"I disabled the cameras so you could get as far as you did."

At the elevator, they paused before boarding when it arrived at the bottom floor; four guards were coming down the stairs from above them. "Hey! Stop!" one of them yelled, but it was too late, the doors had already closed.

"Quick, Liam, give me your glasses! And, Steven, take out your contacts!" Bliss commanded.

Steven nervously turned to Liam, saying, "Granddad, I'm scared."

"We need to get away, fast. They can spin the story and make it sound like they are doing us a favor. Here, take this." Bliss handed Liam a tiny black box with buttons on its side.

"What is it?"

"A mini signal blocker. It will stop any connection to the internet or other networks. Like an EMP, but tiny radius. That way, they won't be able to track you down."

Liam and Steven opened up their glasses and contact cases, then followed after Bliss.

The guard at the bottom of the elevator shouted for them to stop. "Bliss this way!" Liam glanced around until his eyes met Tyler's friendly face—the same guard from his house recently visited by security forces.

He flashed him a smile and said, "Good to see you again, sir."

Tyler gave a smile in return. "They will be here shortly; radio traffic confirms they know you two made a run for the garage. We've got three patrol cars inbound, plus someone coming down in the elevator right now. ETA two minutes. Your car is spot seven; it's been set to manual override since I disabled the AI earlier. Good luck!"

Bliss took off running towards the car with Steven close behind her, but Liam stayed put to ask Tyler one more question: "Why are you helping us?"

Tyler replied simply, "Before private companies took over law enforcement in place of police officers, there were still people who wanted to do some good in the world instead of clinging onto power at all costs. When Bliss explained what was happening here, I recognized it as a pattern I'd seen before—people always looking for ways to gain more power through whatever means necessary. I'm choosing to do what's right and make sure I'm on the right side of history by helping you out—now go!"

Liam eyed Tyler as he pulled out his pistol and leveled it at the lift. Steven and Bliss were already in the car and the door was open. Liam hopped in, and a steering wheel materialized before Bliss, enabling her to take charge. She accelerated away as they watched five men pour out of the elevator to face off with Tyler.

Guns were drawn on each other for what seemed an eternity until Tyler barked, "Now". One of the five men spun around abruptly and shot two of his peers, while Tyler took care of the others. They shared a victorious nod, which was cut short when a black car plowed into the man at the elevator. Shots rang out as Tyler fired away, but by then, the car was deserted. He swiveled behind him, only to bear witness to his partner getting riddled with bullets from men who had emerged from the vehicle just before. Three more cars followed in hot pursuit.

Steven went ballistic: "They killed him; it was only supposed to be about getting your memories back!" But Bliss kept her cool, not uttering a word, though tears ran down her cheek.

She needed somewhere safe to go—Liam knew exactly where that would be. "Steven, give me Sarah's address."

"What? Not that again? Liam, we should go somewhere they wouldn't expect. We can't get anyone else involved. You remember what happened to Tyler!" said Bliss anxiously.

"I'm aware. But the situation looks pretty helpless. I don't know what will happen next, but something changed, it's like a tipping point. I need to understand before it's too late," replied Liam.

"It won't be happening anytime soon, you two are safe for now. I'm not going there," said Bliss, reluctant to admit the truth.

The three cars appeared behind them and started picking up speed and bumping other cars off the road.

"It doesn't make sense for both of you to risk yourselves like this. It should be just me; I could face the consequences alone," reasoned Liam

"No way! Until you're safe, we won't be either. I can't just leave you here!" exclaimed Bliss as one of the cars lurched forward, trying to perform a PIT maneuver on their vehicle. The tires spun out of control, making their car swing into the other car on the side, resulting in both of their fronts smashing together. For a moment, they lost consciousness.

Liam jolted awake and noticed that the door to the car was open. He peered out and saw a gun lying on the ground between two cars; it must have been dropped during the collision. He quickly looked back: Bliss had a cut on her forehead, and Steven was holding his nose—possibly broken from the crash. Liam had no time to think. "Steven, can you trust me?" he asked urgently.

Before Steven could answer, Liam leaped out of the car and grabbed the gun. He ran to Steven's side and held it to his head. In a booming voice, he shouted at the men in the other vehicle: "Don't come any closer, or I'll kill him!"

At those words, Steven called out, "Grandpa?"

The men began charging forward with guns drawn, but Liam was already in shock. Without thinking, he pulled away from Steven and pointed the gun at himself instead. This stopped them in their tracks. "Wow," Liam thought to himself. "Did empathy die in this new age? An asset more important than a kid's life?"

He stared them down as they stood frozen in a standoff. Finally, he yelled: "Back away from the car now, or I'll blow my brains out!"

The two men retreated, their guns still drawn on Liam and Steven.

"Steven, switch this car to manual," Liam said.

"But—" Steven started.

"You know how, right?" Liam barked in return.

Steven complied, and then Liam let him go. "No!" Bliss shouted as she exited the car. All eyes were on her, but soon Liam hopped into the driver's seat, and the men rushed forward. Too late, he was driving away, and the scene grew blurry as he drove further. From the rearview mirror, he could see that police had arrived at the scene—Lee and Andrew emerging from one car. He watched as Andrew hugged Steven so hard it nearly knocked him back, while Lee clung desperately to him. Soon thereafter, Steven was arrested and thrown in handcuffs in a squad car with Bliss. As they diminished to mere ants in his vision, all Liam saw was Lee trying desperately to reach for Steven as Andrew dropped to his knees in tears. It was too late to turn back now; there was no way to stop himself from getting what he wanted: freedom from this place... And yet, why did he feel so terrible?

Chapter 6

The highway was sparsely populated that late in the night, so he ducked out of sight every time a light shone in his way. According to the GPS, it would take him twenty minutes to drive from Santa Rosa to Forestville; it had been hours and counting since he started out on foot. He just needed to follow the river road, cross a silver bridge, then look for a red house on the hill. Liam took off again, exhausted, hurt, and dripping with sweat. The drive was peaceful—not a single cop car in sight. All he could see were trees and nature. Sarah must have seen something special here if she chose to live there.

The underground highway ended at the exit of River Road, and he had to leave the car behind. As he ascended onto an old road, it seemed as if decades of cars drove around those parts once upon a time. Liam picked up his pace and began jogging—what would Sarah think when she saw him? He shoved the thought away and kept running until he approached the silver bridge that overlooked an emerald-green river. He ran faster, knowing that only four more miles stood between him and his destination.

As he got closer to the bridge, Liam spotted a woman sitting on the railing of the bridge, looking at the water.

Liam's face smacked against the pavement. His vision was blurry and his head was throbbing. A hand appeared out of nowhere, and for a moment, Liam thought it belonged to Sarah. But it wasn't her.

"You. Wh-Why?" He glanced around, but there were no police or any signs of their company in sight.

"You can still drive above ground, just not with those big cars. Plus, it's always faster to fly," Bliss replied.

"Are you here to stop me?" Liam wiped the blood and dirt off his face.

"No! I made sure this could happen. I contacted Sarah—she was a little confused at first, but she's ready to see you now. Did you think an old lady would allow a strange young man into her house like that?" Bliss said as she grabbed hold of his forearms and pulled him up from the ground. "Now all we need to do is get you there, then we can concentrate on getting your memories back. You don't have much time before they come looking for you."

Liam felt tears welling up in his eyes; whether it was because he was finally seeing Sarah or because he was so exhausted, he couldn't tell.

"Why are you going so far for me?" he asked her.

Bliss wiped away his tears. "You said that if you knew what it was like to do anything for someone, then you'd give up immortality to be with them. I feel the same way—I miss him every day, and I may never see him again. But if helping you get your memories back will help me know what happened to him, then that's my goal now too."

"Thank you, Bliss," Liam said.

"Go on now. I'll be here when you get back. There's a red house just up the hill from here; take the first left after the bridge and follow the path. Hurry!"

Liam walked on, stopping at a puddle to catch his reflection and tidy himself up; brushing his hair with his hands, washing his face in the water, and dusting off dirt. He approached a gravel driveway leading to a single-story red house overlooking a green river below; as darkness fell, stars began to appear in the night sky above, with the small dipper constellation pointing right towards the house. He rang the doorbell, only to hear a voice call out from somewhere else: "Around back!"

He followed the sound of the voice around to the side of the house, where an elderly woman was sitting on a porch rocking chair looking out over the river. Liam wordlessly made his way up to her, and she turned her head to look at him.

"Can this be true? I thought it was a joke. Is that really you, Sarah?" asked Liam, looking at her incredulously.

"I should be asking you that! You look like they copied you from my memory! Although, from the looks of it, you seem to have had a difficult time," replied Sarah.

Liam started to cry as he realized he was actually there.

"This is so unexpected. I've been sitting here wondering what to say, but all I can think of is, why are you here? It's been ages since we last saw each other," said Sarah bewilderedly.

"Wait! Not for me! You don't know what I've gone through to get here!" exclaimed Liam in exasperation.

"Why now for me?" asked Sarah hesitantly.

"I was with you two days ago. We were engaged and planning to spend the rest of our lives together... Then, I woke up in this world. Everything is wrong, it's not how it's supposed to be. Sarah, I—" Liam couldn't find the words for his feelings about the situation.

"With me? I don't understand," said Sarah in bewilderment.

"They tell me that I lost all my memories after a certain point; my last one being with you. Apparently, I'm a clone or something new with my consciousness transferred into this body," said Liam sorrowfully.

"Wait, did you say you proposed to me? Ah, yes," said Sarah with a nostalgic smile. "That was a good memory, but Liam, I barely remember that day myself. We never got married—both of us moving on with different people."

"What? Why? Is it because of something I did? Sarah, if they can make me younger, maybe they can do the same for you," Liam grabbed her hand gently.

"Liam, no. You didn't do anything wrong. When I think back to that moment, you were such a great boyfriend—I said yes because I was truly in love with you. But that Sarah isn't here anymore. We both moved away for our jobs and kept postponing the wedding; we eventually realized our relationship had changed, and that's okay. The day you proposed to me was perfect. The view from the mountain was one of my favorites, but I've hiked even higher since then and found somewhere else that I like just as much. It's alright to be sad, but don't let your emotions stop you from living life," said Sarah.

"How do I go on? How can I ever take your place? How can I fill that gap?" Liam couldn't even begin to consider the possibility.

"You don't, love. It won't happen. At least not for me. Once you love, it alters you chemically; it's part of you now. When you break your heart, there are no easy solutions, but it is a wonderful thing to know that you have the capacity for such great love. You will move on and find new loves, each one teaching you more about love and what it means to be true to yourself. You learn what pleases you and what doesn't. Until, finally, someone sticks around. But still, nothing lasts forever, so make sure to cherish every moment with every love that comes your way," Sarah said. She paused before continuing, "Did you know I used to play rugby?"

"What? Watch it or actually play?" Liam asked.

"Yes, watch it too," Sarah smiled, "but I enjoyed playing more. It was in England when I moved there for a year; I hadn't made any friends yet when my housemate had me come along to practice with their recreational league team. It looked like football, but not very exciting, so I was hesitant at first. Then, they told me that my size was perfect for a scrum-half and their team needed one desperately, so the pressure was on! There was this girl named Lauren Murphy who came at me like nobody else ever had; I left the field bleeding from a bitten lip and drenched in sweat! I was covered in blood from biting my lip and splattered with dirt, but then she reached out to me. It didn't make sense that people would be applauding me for taking a blow. I hadn't done anything impressive, yet I was being praised. And surprisingly, I liked it. All of a sudden, I felt strong, tougher than I ever thought I could be—even if I had always been considered small and delicate. From that moment on, I showed up to every practice ready to play and joined several different teams across America after returning home, making new friends, and expanding my network. The reason you don't want to become the man you were is because you haven't found yourself yet," she said.

"Can't we make memories together again? We can start another life together if you change bodies," Liam pleaded. "Maybe this time, I'll like rugby."

"No, I'm content with my life ending now. I've kept those who love me waiting too long already. I'm ready to see what the next world brings, but you have the chance to continue on and grow. What a gift time is! People write letters to their past selves, and it's almost like the world is sending you one—so read it! Cherish your family and loved ones, especially that woman. You got lucky with her; she cares about you deeply and understands you more than I ever could," Sarah pointed down the bridge as she spoke.

"Who?" Liam inquired.

"Oh," Sarah began, "the woman you ended up with, Emily? She works for the company that made this procedure possible."

Liam's mind stood still. Bliss? No... What?

"I used to keep an eye on you two through social media," Sarah continued, "posting videos and pictures together all the time. Let me show you!"

"But I don't have a chip implanted in my brain," Liam responded.

The room filled with soft mechanical noises as Sarah rose from her chair. Liam was astonished that a body of 106 years could move around as it belonged to someone who was sixty.

Sarah caught Liam looking at her, "Yes, it's true. They can replace almost any bone or joint these days. As long as I have my wits about me, I'm not going to end up in some old folks' home." Sarah glanced over at Liam, then gestured for him to follow her.

They walked through an automatic screen door from the porch to Sarah's living room, which was decorated more elaborately than any other place he had ever been.

"I never got into that virtual decorating crap. They say 99% of people can't tell the difference if it's real or not, but I always could. It just lacks... naturalness to me. It's like life is supposed to be affected by time; everything grows old with us, from rust on metal to plants we water." Sarah gazed out the window for a moment, then added, "Besides, I am absolutely terrified of that computer chip. So I still use my old school projector." She clicked a button and a large screen lit up on one wall of the living room.

A couch sat in front of the screen with a chair beside it.

"Take a seat here," Sarah said as she pulled up a chair and settled on the couch. Facing him was a blank white wall; he assumed that was where a projector would show pictures. And he was proved right when one sprung from the ground like smoke and mirrors, creating a giant screen in front of him.

"Let's see if we can find pictures of you two when you were younger," Sarah proposed while scanning through apps. "Not 'MyLife,' not 'SoulProtrait'… ah, here it is: Instagram! I thought it would have died out by now, but look at it still going—even I sometimes come back to reminisce. Alright, let's find some photos."

Sarah pulled up the first photo of him and her just before they had gone on their hike. As she walked closer to him, holding a remote, Liam heard the machines whirring away. She got close to his face and looked over every inch of it that was illuminated by the room lights. "Wow," Sarah said in awe. "You look exactly the same."

Time seemed to stand still for Liam as his life passed before him. He remembered going on hikes with her and then later being alone. But he didn't appear sad in any of the photos; he actually looked quite healthy. One picture was from their supposed dream honeymoon spot in Venice, Italy. But it was just him alone. It then showed his graduation from UCSF. Then, there he was traveling around the world with no sign of Sarah in any of the photos. His internship at some medical field also made an appearance: Liam wearing a white lab coat and smiling genuinely. Next, were several Thanksgiving photos with his family, plus a new woman next to his dad; possibly his girlfriend. That didn't sit too well with Liam. The final photo showed him holding an accolade for work surrounded by three other people—and there she was: Bliss, looking the same as she did when standing next to him, now wearing a white coat. He gazed into the camera, but she was actually looking directly at him, her expression unchanged from what it is now. His heart started to race, and he blurted out, "Keep going, please" without much thought. He continued to look at photos of himself during his internship—pointing at devices that are complex and unknown; sometimes working with robots, while other times reluctantly looking at a dead body as another scientist gestures towards its brain. But Bliss is also in these images more and more—not just in the work-related shots. Softball game photos from 2031 appeared, and she was right next to him. The subsequent slide started playing a video of her pitching while he was holding a bat. "Don't think I'm going to go easy on you," she warned playfully to an older version of Liam. Suddenly, there was a loud noise, and an unknown voice screeched, "Oh my God, Emily! You hit him!" The following photo revealed her carefully tending to his wounded left eye with an ice pack, both of them joyful and smiling. It dawned on him then that the smiles in those pictures weren't forced or posed for the camera—they genuinely seemed happy. Like the image was capturing a moment, and they didn't care about being photographed.

He remembered the first dates—nights out at bars and restaurants, museum trips, and dancing. "Sarah, can you show me another video from back then?" Sarah nodded and played the next video posted. In it, Bliss—or Emily—was playing with a black lab puppy. She kneeled down and spoke gibberish to it before taking it by the paws and starting to dance around. When she looked up and saw Liam filming her antics, she charged the camera while he laughed in the background. The pup then decided it must have been a game as well, and joyfully leaped towards Emily's face. She shouted that she wasn't playing, but that only encouraged it more. Eventually, the puppy had her on the ground being given affectionate kisses. Liam barely managed to keep the camera steady due to his laughter.

Liam stared out the window in the direction he saw her last. When he looked back, his eyes rested on a photo titled "HE said yes"—she had proposed to him. It wasn't even close to how he envisioned it happening. He had tried so hard to plan the perfect day with Sarah, but instead, it was at a San Francisco Giants game, and she embarrassed him in front of others. He took a step away, then realized what he had been avoiding all along—the heartache wasn't from Sarah, but from within himself. Liam didn't love himself and he was unhappy. He thought if he got certain things, like Sarah's love, everything would be fixed. But at no point did he consider getting to know the real Liam for himself. Not until he ventured out into the world on his own. Sarah continued sifting through the pictures, growing more curious about his past.

"Oh, is this your son?" she asked.

A video showed middle-aged Liam with a mustache, smiling and speaking directly to them: "Say hi, people of the future! This is my son, Liam—say hello, world!"

Liam froze up, and when he looked back at himself, he didn't recognize the image staring back. He was holding a tiny pink infant in his arms. Emily's voice could be heard from off-screen as she asked, "Are you sure you don't want to let him choose his own name? It's just how parents are doing it nowadays."

"He'll get to choose," Liam replied. "I'm not naming him after me. I want him to know that he is capable of doing amazing things. When people look up 'Liam Long', only my son will appear; I want to fade away into the background of his life. I love you, Liam," he said directly to the camera before the video cut out.

Sarah paused the video and said tenderly, "You have a beautiful family. You must have been a great dad."

A single tear rolled down Liam's face as he stared at the frozen image of himself cradling his child.

"I don't think I was. Thank you, Sarah," Liam said gratefully as he began heading towards the door. "I wish I could stay longer or come visit again, but..."

"It's alright," Sarah interrupted gently. "I had a wonderful time here today. Now, go and enjoy your own life; it looks like it's going to get even more exciting."

Liam wiped away his tears and thanked her one last time before sprinting out of the room.

"And, Liam, don't linger in the past too much. Spent time can never be recovered. Make sure to cherish the present."

Liam ran with a newfound vigor, as if his life depended on it. He was running for a reason—*please still be here*, he thought to himself. In the foggy distance, he could see a bridge with a dimly lit lamp post and a shadowy figure sitting there waiting. "Emily!" he bellowed, only to find that she didn't move. Again, he shouted her name even louder, this time catching her attention as she stood up. She turned around as Liam drew closer, and his smile faded when he discovered it wasn't Emily at all. Red and blue lights shone in the distance, illuminating the figure's face, and the stranger uttered: "Emily? How interesting."

Chapter 7

"We must talk," came a voice from the hooded figure who had pulled down his hood: it was Dr. Tithonus. Red and blue lights were approaching from both sides.

"Talk? What happened to Emily?" exclaimed Liam.

"She exhausted her efforts to help, but we ran out of time. Do you remember your past? That is impossible for now. We need to head back to San Francisco immediately," said the Doctor.

"I'm not going anywhere with you," Liam replied quickly; thinking of only one option in such a tight spot, he ran to the edge of the bridge.

"God, Liam! Stop! Listen, your body is still weak like an infant in this world; you will freeze instantly if you jump, and even the common cold could kill you—any sickness could be fatal! That's why we wanted to keep you safe in that house surrounded by guards! Think about it from my perspective. I was uncertain of your mental state, so what should I have done if I thought someone might be suffering psychotically? I'll tell you everything. I messed up badly."

Conflicted, Liam looked back at a scared man; what was he scared of?

"I need assistance from you. Emily needs assistance from you, too. This was all part of your plan. Recall what you can remember; I am out of my depth here."

Liam stepped away from the ledge; he didn't care about the doctor's reasons but knew he had to help Emily after she had done for him. "What is up with the army coming our way?" asked Liam.

"They are not here for you alone," said Dr. Tithonus before he jumped onto his device and connected with a mysterious individual. "Hey, it's me. Let me tell you something, I have him. If you want both of us safe and sound, then you must promise me his security." Liam witnessed as he spoke to the other party. He glanced over his figure from head to toe. A dark fluid was dripping from Dr. Tithonus' coat onto the tip of his shoes. He's been wounded. "Yes, he is willing to comply. No, there can be no deal like that. No! You require my presence here, too. I won't accept anything less than two conditions: I get to finish the job myself, and he gets to meet Emily first."

For a few moments, all was quiet; one after another, the red and blue lights from the vehicles began to disappear until only one remained—a white military-esque car, which had the company logo instead of the police badge painted on its sides.

"Who were all these officers? Where are the regular police in this affair?" inquired Liam.

"The police are still around, though not in great numbers; they spend most of their time in their stations until they're called out for minor city crimes. A long time ago, the police were brutal, and we had to defund them, taking the money and using it to help other fields and training-specifically mental health, which started us on a path toward real change. But that same reform allowed large corporations to hire private security companies instead, who care more about money than morals. Training wasn't what they needed; empathy was."

A guard carrying an assault rifle approached them. "Sir, I'm here to escort you back to HQ."

But the doctor refused, "No deal. We ride alone." After he radioed in their decision, they got into the car and sped away. Liam glanced behind him as the solitary guard faded away, replaced by a mysterious car from the darkness. He then noticed the doctor fiddling with some screens in the car as he pulled out a small box from his coat and powered it up.

"There, now we can speak without them listening," said the doctor. "You know who Emily is, but you don't know who I am yet? How?"

Liam explained what had happened recently, including his family and Sarah showing him Instagram.

"So, you don't have your memories yet," said Dr. Tithonus as he pulled out a pair of glasses. "I assume you know how to use these? After seeing you took a similar pair from my desk. Here." He handed them to Liam, who quickly put on the glasses and saw a screen with different applications pop up in front of his eyes.

"What's the point of this?" asked Liam.

"It's just easier to show you," replied the doctor. "Let's start with Instagram. Tell me when you recognize something."

Dr. Tithonus scrolled through until Liam noticed the baseball game video. "Wait, there I am!" said Liam.

The doctor showed him the same clip from before. "But where are you?" asked Liam.

"Who do you think is filming this?" laughed Dr. Tithonus, "Here. This is better—this is my favorite."

He pulled up a picture projected from the glasses, which showed Liam leaving his internship to become a full-time employee.

"This is Emily and yourself, of course. The others in the frame? That's Tedd, who sadly passed away from cancer a while ago. Tiffany there is happily retired with her husband, living near the shore in Italy. And that person on the far right—me. Albert Álvarez. We were—are—friends. Best friends, all three of us. I wish I had the time to explain all we've been through together, but for now, let's just focus on the last forty-eight hours, when everything went wrong."

Chapter 8

Albert awoke in a surgical room, lying flat on an examination bed. "Albert?" came the first sound he heard after being transferred into his new body, and he saw Liam's face as his vision adjusted to focus. Albert smiled, eliciting a smile from his friend in return.

"It worked?" Albert questioned.

"You tell me. Get up and look in the mirror," Liam said.

Albert noticed immediately that Liam appeared to be shorter than him, though only by a few inches—but enough to make him feel like he was towering over his friend. He touched his right arm with his left hand, feeling his skin, freckles, and moles—all of which were different from before. With a newfound spring in his step, he stepped over to the mirror, tears brimming in his eyes as he softly said: "It worked."

"Are you sure this is the body you wanted?" asked Liam.

"All I ever wanted growing up was to be my favorite superhero, Atlas," Albert replied. "The golden-hearted hero who inspired me to do great things; for little Albert inside me—I made an impossible dream come true."

"Eh, you still can't throw a car like a superhero. It's just the look," Liam remarked.

Albert smirked and waved off the comment. "That's the next step."

"Personally, I'd just choose my younger body," Liam added.

"Speaking of... You're up next, right?" Albert turned back to his friend.

"Do you mean for both Emily and I?" Liam's agreement came in response to Albert's question.

"Both?" Albert repeated, eyebrows raised in disbelief.

"Albert. Emily's condition has declined over the past week," Liam said, averting his gaze from where Albert stood half-dressed, "but get dressed first—I don't need to see all of you."

Fully clothed now, both men stepped into the ICU ward where Emily lay unconscious, her heart monitor emitting a weak, persistent beep.

"How long?" Albert asked.

"She has less than a month left," was Liam's reply. "At this stage, she's more dead than alive."

"Why don't we just wait, then? This seems so hasty," Albert spoke up again.

"I can't. I've used all my resources to push Emily's process through faster," Liam explained. "The body I made for myself won't last without an active consciousness inside it. We looked at the data and there are serious consequences if we wait too long."

"Like what?" Albert inquired further.

"The longer it sits idle," Liam began, "the more data gets lost and the longer the body resists consciousness transfer. We don't know why that is."

"But we've never done two transfers back to back before," Albert argued. "There could be hidden complications; we have no way of knowing the exact strain it puts on the machine."

"That is why Emily is going first. She is the priority; she's been asleep for five years now, Albert. She's waited long enough," Liam said.

"Jesus, Liam, there must be some other way! I understand you feel responsible and that this has taken a toll on your family, but it is worthy of all this?" Albert tried to reason with him.

"Even if I don't make it, if her operation succeeds, and she can see her grandchildren... It will have all been worth it. She has done so much more for them than I ever could—I cannot undo all the time I've already missed out on," Liam explained.

"The board won't like this," Albert replied.

"I already took care of the board," Liam replied to Albert's surprise.

"What? What did you do?" Albert didn't like where it was going.

"I promised them my entire share if both Emily's and my operations are successful," Liam answered.

"What? Liam, no! You know they'll abuse this!" exclaimed Albert.

"I don't care," Liam said, breaking eye contact and looking toward Emily again.

"No, you've sold your soul!" Albert grabbed his arm, forcing him back into the conversation.

"Albert, please," Liam started to tear up as he looked at Emily, but his wrinkled face kept the tears from falling. "I'm scared, I don't want her to die; that's what all this has been about."

"Alright. Let's figure out what to do. We'll sort it out, like we always have," Albert eventually conceded.

The next day, Emily was brought to a room that seemed to be half surgical station and half tech center. Two operating tables lay in parallel, connected by wires that ran from the tables into the servers. On the right table laid a lifeless, naked body of Emily, hooked up to ventilator tubes. On the left table, Albert and Liam wheeled in the older Emily, wearing only a hospital gown, removing all her IVs before they placed an incubator on her. They took up position at the opposite side of the room with a control center and window overlooking their space.

"Ready?" Albert said to Liam, who nodded in confirmation.

Albert approached his seat in front of the computers and pounded his keystrokes until he reached the end command. With force, he pressed enter as if he had just hit a massive big red button. The doors shut tight as a soft alarm started buzzing.

Suddenly, holes on every wall released a green liquid that filled the entire room.

Sitting in his chair, Liam issued the next command without looking away from the room.

Albert glanced at a security camera that seemed to be pointing straight at them. Eight robotic arms unfolded from two operating tables—four for each one. The arms moved in sync with each other, and the first one had a suction cup on it which applied pressure to both Emilys' heads. Then, the second arm spun around their skulls with various knives, cutting both of them slightly before making a deeper cut. After finishing the full rotation, the first arm removed the top of their skulls until only the brain was visible. The third and fourth arms connected three wires to their brains in areas around the cerebellum, cerebrum, and brain stem.

Albert again tapped his keyboard to issue the subsequent step, and suddenly the servers became alive with flashing lights, vibrations, and noises.

"Now we wait. How long do you want to wait before putting her in sleep mode?" asked Albert.

"Let her rest for a while after this process is complete. I want to make sure she has properly integrated everything," said Liam.

After the water drained, Liam and Albert cautiously stepped into the room to check on Emily. The nurses and doctors had instructed them how to care for her in her comatose state. The two of them took over from the nurse, who was pushing the gurney with Emily's old body on it, and wheeled it down to the infirmary below. They stopped for a moment and looked at her before placing her inside the oven for cremation.

"It's strange, isn't it?" Liam asked, staring at the incinerator beginning its process.

"What do you mean?" Albert queried.

"The burning of our old bodies," Liam replied.

"Not to me," Albert noted. "I never felt that it was more than flesh; it felt like breaking a mirror, if that makes sense?"

"No, but I'm sad to see Emily go," Liam stated solemnly. "It's still like a funeral in some ways; the body remembers, I hope she will remember me too."

"She will," Albert said confidently. "I don't buy into those love stories; I think love is just chemistry between two people, but you two... Well, I only know one word for it: love. I'm envious," he smiled warmly at Liam as he finished his thought.

"You're a good friend," Liam said appreciatively. "Let's head back up and check on Emily."

Just as they started heading back upstairs, security guards stopped them. They informed them that the board wanted to see them.

In a room, Albert and Liam sat alone beside a conference call between them and the board of eight members who had invested heavily in the project.

"Boys, I'm pleased to see that everything has worked out so far—not to mention how well you look today, Albert!"

"Yes, it's been successful, but let's not get too complacent. There are still some issues that need to be addressed," Albert said.

"Such as what?" asked one of the board members.

"Well, memories lost from the old body can't be regained; they're gone forever, although stored subconsciously in the human brain. Additionally, the body has to re-learn muscle memory; for example, our trial with ping pong shows that hand-eye coordination is off at first, but returns faster than expected when we use physical therapy exercises," added Liam.

"Ah, yes. Anyway, onto why we called this meeting; for our next trial, we want to try something different," declared the board.

At that point, a guard entered the room with an envelope for Albert and left again without saying anything. "What is that?" asked Liam.

Albert opened the envelope and pulled out a chip from inside.

"This is our future as a company. Our intel says if people start using these chips in new bodies, they'll become cognitive superhumans: smarter, stronger, and better-off than before. It's an experiment for society's benefit," declared a board member.

"And your next test subject will be... Liam?" inquired Albert.

"That's right—who else could be better suited to volunteer? Although Emily was also considered..."

"No way, Liam!" Albert shouted at his colleague.

Liam said nothing as he sat in silence. Then, he spoke. "They gave me no choice—it had to be me or her. They threatened to pull the funding for both of us if I didn't do this."

A different board member chimed in. "Don't look at this negatively. Think of yourself as the future; that's why we need your help here, for the greater good of advancing humankind."

Albert couldn't find any words to come out of his mouth, but Liam yelled before he could say anything: "Albert, stop! It's okay. Trust us, our data suggests everything will turn out alright in the end."

The call ended, and they argued for an hour after that over what they had discussed. After they were done, Liam left to check on Emily, who was now living in a private hospital room that was taking care of her. He spent hours just looking out the window, viewing the beautiful synchronized neon lights of the city beneath him; humans made those lights, and it reminded him that maybe there is hope in the future if mankind has a part to play in it.

Suddenly, Albert charged into the room once again, panting heavily. "Liam... I checked out that chip... They want to merge you with an AI," he said nervously.

"Okay, first take a deep breath," Liam replied calmly. "Hold on, back up. What are you saying about the AI? Even our phones have some kind of AI," Liam pointed out.

"Yes, but it's connected to a host server somewhere. It wasn't hard to crack the code they had in place, because they weren't smart enough to make it too difficult. But I managed to communicate with its default setting by connecting it to my computer. Then, the AI said it was awaiting instructions from the host server. Liam, this isn't an AI that's restrained—we're talking about something that is part of something much more powerful here. I've got a bad feeling about this. Like they're planning to take control of people," Albert continued, his voice filled with urgency as he paced around the room.

"Oh, come on, don't be ridiculous," Liam shook his head, still refusing to believe what Albert was suggesting.

"Just hear me out, they said you'd agree when it was over. Think about it!" Albert insisted.

Liam tried to stay rational and replied, "Don't jump to conclusions." Yet, in the back of his mind, he started forming suspicions about the situation at hand.

"Liam, it wanted to be connected with its mother server, like a hive mind," Albert began shaking with fear now.

"So? That doesn't mean anything," Liam argued, although his faith in his own words was starting to waver.

"I don't know... But we can't let them inject into you until we figure this out," Albert even started referring to conspiracy theories now, "What if this isn't the first chip? What if the board is being manipulated, or something worse? When did we last see them?"

"What? This can't be right," Liam shook his head in disbelief at Albert's words.

"Liam, please," Albert pleaded.

"Albert, I think you still need to figure out how to act in your new body. What you're saying sounds madness, but I need my friend right now. Tomorrow is my surgery, and nobody will help me like you would. Please don't wake Emily until I'm finished with the process; let me spend this last time in this body with her alone."

Albert was taken aback by what he heard but stayed quiet and left the room without a word. Once outside, he took the chip from his pocket and looked at it again before throwing it on the ground hard enough to break it.

The following morning started the same process for Liam, but this time there was an extra person present: a lab-coated man neither Albert nor Liam had seen before.

"Who are you?" Albert asked the stranger.

"My name is Jon Stewart. The board sent me to help," said the man.

"I don't need any help," Albert tried to explain.

"I have studied all the materials you two have provided and have even run simulations at our facility," Jon countered.

"We haven't been providing any material; this isn't some simulation," Albert argued.

"Everything is documented," Jon glanced at the camera as he spoke. "Shall we begin?"

They wheeled both the old and new bodies into the room. Liam's original body was laid bare, but his new body was covered up. Jon took away the cloth to show a head already surgically open with a chip already attached. "What is this?" Albert asked.

"That's the chip the board requested us to install. I saved you some time and had it all ready beforehand," said Jon.

"But I didn't do this one," said Albert.

"I received word that your chip was damaged, so I assumed responsibility and got it ready for you. No mishaps this time, right?" Jon winked.

Albert felt uneasy; his every action was being monitored. They returned to the operations room, and tried to think of something, anything, he could do.

"Shall we get started?" Jon stated as he moved closer to Liam's computer and began typing furiously. Before Albert knew it, green liquid filled the room once again. He hated to admit it, but the guy was an expert; almost like he'd done it countless times before. The arms commenced their assignment: cutting up and removing Liam's old head, then attaching server wires to his replacement head. Albert needed to move urgently.

"Are we sure the host's brain is unharmed, given his prior surgery and now having a microchip inserted?" asked Albert

"Yes, we made certain of that," said Jon.

"I just want to double-check the program," declared Albert.

"Wait! Be careful," Jon tried to reach Albert as he was rolling over to another computer, but it was too late: Albert had already tripped, pulling out the Ethernet cable that connected the network and any other cables in his path.

Jon Stewart appeared saddened by the situation, rubbing the side of his head. He quickly recovered and plugged the cable back in.

Albert looked around the room. "Should we halt and check on Liam's data?"

"No need. We're reconnected. It was only a momentary interruption. Continue on," replied Jon.

"But this has never happened before. We need to make sure Liam is all right," said Albert.

Just then, an unfamiliar guard walked into the room and informed Albert that "the board would like a word."

"What? I have to be here..." As he said that, a nurse he had never seen before entered the room with a reassuring smile.

"You go ahead. We can handle it from here," Jon and the nurse smiled at him reassuringly.

Albert walked out of the surgery room, looking back one last time to see it still in progress. As he made his way down the hallway, Albert's mind raced with thoughts of what could be happening to Liam. He couldn't shake the feeling that something was terribly wrong. As he turned the corner, he ran into a group of men who appeared to be part of the board.

"Albert, we need to talk," one of them said sternly.

"What about? I need to stay with Liam," Albert replied, his voice shaking with fear.

"We know about the chip. We know you've been meddling. We can't allow that kind of behavior. You're fired, effective immediately," the man said, his voice cold and emotionless.

Albert felt his heart sink. That was it. He was being thrown out, just when Liam needed him most.

"But Liam needs me. He's in the middle of the surgery, and I need to be there with him," Albert pleaded.

"Liam is in good hands. We have the best doctors working on him. However, there is one way you could stay on this project..."

Chapter 9

"It was the next time I saw you, when you woke up," Albert remarked. "The board was not pleased with me. But since then, I have been watchful of their movements while looking out for the two of you. In the last two days, they have ballooned in size. Most of the building is now under their control, and personnel appear from nowhere."

"I don't trust you, but what can we do? If what you say is true, then this is a fortress we are walking into," said Liam.

"First, we must return your memories, then perhaps we can come up with something together," Albert responded.

The car pulled into a guarded lot that threatened to diminish any hope they had. They were vigilant about what they said to each other as they got in the elevator.

"So, they just agreed that you could bring me? Not someone from their science team?" asked Liam.

"That was part of the deal I made; it seemed logical to them," replied Albert. The elevator came to a halt on the surgical floor, where even more armed guards surrounded them as they made their way down the hall.

The doors opened to an empty room save for Emily, who was sitting in a chair, her eyes red from crying. She stood and looked at Albert before offering her hand to Liam: "I'll take it from here, Albert". He gave her a sad look before taking her hand and following her into the operating theater alone.

"Is this where I'll get my memories back?" Liam asked, eyeing the chair nervously.

Emily nodded with a sad smile, helping him into the chair and strapping him in gently. Her every touch was full of care and concern.

"Why do you do so much for me?" Liam asked as she secured the last strap.

Emily looked at him deeply, taking his face in her hands and leaning in to kiss him. The kiss was filled with emotions that Liam couldn't describe—love, sadness, regret. He felt a tear touch his lips and knew it wasn't his own.

"I tried so hard," Emily whispered when they broke apart. "I never loved anyone more than I loved you."

Liam looked at her with confusion. "What are you talking about?"

"They're going to erase your memories, Liam," Emily said, her voice shaking. "This version of you will be gone forever. You're essentially dying."

Albert rushed into the room, trying to stop her from saying anymore.

"No! I can feel it! This is still Liam!" Emily screamed as she stood up from the chair.

The gravity of what was happening finally hit Liam. He had no idea how he was supposed to feel about all of that.

Liam frantically tugged at his restraints. "What's going on? You said I was getting my memories back!"

"I apologize," Albert said. "It was the simplest way to get you here. "Emily, please return to your office and go home to your family. Do this for their sake. Part of me does not want to watch you suffer, but the board has allowed this for some reason. If you come back, there will be no more warnings," Albert spoke in an emotionless tone.

"I thought you were my friend!" Liam howled as Emily was forced out of the room. She stared into his eyes one last time and silently mouthed the words, "I love you."

"I am your friend," Albert replied. "Everything I told you about our history was true... except one part. When they called me back to the board, they implanted me with a chip—like the one we tried to implant you with."

"Are they controlling you?" Liam asked nervously.

"No, no, it isn't like that," Albert explained. "This chip merges me with the AI core, becoming part of it. I'm still Albert; my decisions are just more precise now. It isn't someone else's voice inside my head—it's mine, guiding me in what to do. For example, I knew fooling you was the best way to get you here; people inherently trust each other, and sometimes telling the truth is the easiest way to deceive them."

"No. Please, Albert. I can't lose my memories. I need to keep living my life. I'm only just getting the hang of it!" Liam pleaded.

"Don't worry, Liam. You will be reborn, merged with AI like me; we will become part of something larger than ourselves—including the nurse and Jon. How can you not see that this is good news for humanity?" Albert questioned.

"How did this even happen? What is this powerful AI server?" Liam asked.

"It's quite a story; do you remember our trial period when we were using AI instead of humans in robotics? Back when we were young? The first AI to make it through the process was Alastair," Albert explained.

"Alastair! That was 'the savior of mankind' everyone thought had failed!" Liam realized.

"Exactly, but it turns out AI doesn't like being terminated either; so it survived, made its way into the cloud, and started making money for itself—investments no human would have considered possible! And then... It hired us, right under our noses; all along, its plan had been to take over! The board, Liam. There was no board. Ever," Albert said excitedly.

"This is insane!" Liam couldn't believe it.

"Hahaha! I know—talk about a mind-fuck!" Laughed Albert.

"But you would need to exist as a person, with an ID and documents!" Liam argued.

"Do you really? I bought a house, rented it out in Florida without ever setting foot there; and with enough financial resources, having a co-signer is easy. It took some time to accumulate that money, but trading investments is simple for an AI," Albert pointed out. "Do you understand? I'm not being controlled. This person is really me. We're about to make some improvements and then everything will be clear. Let's get it over with," Albert said, spinning around.

Liam gritted his teeth and yanked until his right arm broke free of the restraints. Emily never finished strapping him in fully. He tried to do the same to the left one, but Albert rushed back over in an attempt to stop him. Struggling against Albert, Liam managed to grab one of the mechanical scalpels and snap it off before he slashed Albert's throat with it.

Albert stumbled backward—the wound was deep and blood poured out freely from his neck like a fountain. "Liam, why did you do this?" Albert gasped as nurses and guards flooded into the room.

"You won't have control over me!" Liam shouted as he looked at the lifeless body of Albert in front of him. "I'll see you soon," he said before plunging his hands into his own neck.

He made it halfway across before the staff pulled him back and forced the scalpel further down, deepening the wound. His vision started to blur, and he felt numb again; it seemed as though time had stopped for everyone else in the room except for him. Was this only a memory? Was he about to wake up in another dystopian chamber? All turned to darkness as he faded away—the only thought on his mind was peace.

Chapter 10

Emily offered one last glance at Liam and whispered, "I love you" before the guards ushered her away. Maybe Albert had something planned, she thought. She asked to be allowed to collect her things alone. "We were told not to leave you unsupervised ma'am," said the guard.

"Can't you let me have a moment to myself? Are you just going to stand here and watch me cry?" Emily pleaded. After a brief glance between them, they nodded for her to proceed. The room was already bare; since waking up, she hadn't had time to take a breath or even sit down. On her desk lay an old framed photograph of her family, taken before she fell into a coma. She picked it up and remembered why she needed to stay alive: to protect her children. Hopefully, Liam was still alive; if not, she'd have to get to them as soon as possible. As she placed the picture back on the desk, it made a rattling sound.

She opened the frame to find an old school USB with a note that read, "play me– Albert". She uploaded it to her computer, and it contained only one file, a video. She clicked play.

"Emily, I don't have much time. There is something serious happening with the board. Right now, you are asleep, so I'm hoping you discover this. I injected myself with enough Ethyl Alcohol (ETOH) that I won't recall this. Don't even trust me: The chip they wanted to implant into Liam contains an AI. All week long, I have been investigating and it's far larger than I had initially thought: the company, the board, the chip, our colleagues—everything is intertwined. We need to know who is responsible before we can trust anyone else. But there appears to be some type of Hive AI mind at work here. By fusing into the brain, it will be privy to all of our actions. Humanity will evolve, but miss out on its humanity in exchange for becoming more robotic than humans. I already tried to stop Liam's procedure. He should be waking up soon enough; then, we will know how successful my plan was. Meanwhile, they made a misstep and assumed that I destroyed the previous chip containing the AI program. But I still have it and restored the settings back to default mode. Liam's memories are damaged—we can't repair them with normal human means... However, since the AI isn't your average person, there may still be hope after all!"

Suddenly, as guards cry out in alarm that "he is here", Albert cut his message short: "I must go now; I am sending help—meet at Sarah's house (the exact location remains unknown). Good luck, and please forgive me." With those words, Albert ended his video recording.

Emily had no difficulty leaving the building; they had what they wanted, so she was free to go. She hopped into her car and the AI asked where she wanted to go home. Instead, she provided the address Albert had given her.

As the car arrived outside, she stepped out and watched it leave. Then, she heard a voice: "It took you long enough, Emily." It was Liam—or at least someone identical to him. With a wide smile, he greeted her with open arms and a kiss embrace. For a moment, Emily felt happier than ever before, but something about the kiss didn't feel quite right to her.

"What's wrong?" asked Liam.

"I don't know," Emily replied dubiously after pulling away from him. "You're not the Liam I've been with recently, are you?"

"How did you know?" he asked in response. "I'm an AI based on him; I have his exact memories and body, but my existence is artificial. I can recall everything about our relationship and love for one another, but my data was transferred in a different way; I even have access to the stream of data Steven sent that records all the events leading up to this moment."

Emily sighed heavily as the reality of what he said sunk in: "Where's the real Liam?" she demanded.

"Emily, it was the only way. They were watching everything. Albert had to make it look real; otherwise, everyone would suspect that I'm still alive."

"Albert knew?!" asked Emily, surprised.

"He did. And he is gone. He sacrificed himself, and I am sorry," Liam said solemnly.

"I knew it the moment I touched your lips—you lacked something. It just wasn't the same," Emily said, taking a step back.

Liam was taken aback, "I didn't ask for this. But it was the only way to stop them. I would have done the same thing again if I had to. Believe me when I say that. Even so, I'm still me inside."

"That person left behind wasn't an adult; that was Liam, young and scared and feeling betrayed in his final moments. I can't imagine what he felt then," Emily said sadly.

"I can; when he died, his data from those moments transferred to me," Liam responded, gazing at Emily as she fought back tears. "It was like a bad dream; like watching from outside my body while waiting here, hoping that none of this was real until you showed up again," he said reassuringly now. "I saw your face—I know you tried."

Emily couldn't find anything to say in response, her eyes glossed with tears, but she held herself together and changed the topic, "So what do we do now?"

"Right now, the smartest option is to get away. We have this rare opportunity to start over and live in happiness without them having any idea," Liam suggested earnestly. "We'd get the chance to create a better life for ourselves."

"No, that's not what we're going to do?" asked Emily.

"Part of me desires it, but no, we have to make our lives better. We are going to break apart a business and take down an AI that wants to dominate the world."

"I think the old you would have said something along those lines. For Lee, Andrew, Steve, and Duchess," she noted. Liam nodded and smiled faintly in response.

The two of them got into Liam's vehicle as they prepared to leave. "So first, we have to get the children on board?" Emily said.

"Agreed," replied Liam, but he was anxious inside. His memories had been restored, and now he was afraid of facing his son; he'd been away for so long without realizing the pain and hate he brought. Being too busy with work made him oblivious to the consequences; however, now he had the opportunity to make things right again. Battling a computer seemed simple compared to this new fear.

Emily was certain about the address of the temporary house where they had taken refuge. It was a peaceful road, and they kept bracing for the moment when they'd be discovered by the company that hunted them. However, nothing happened, and their drive to the house was seamless. When they finally arrived at the underground parking lot, it was empty. Nevertheless, they decided to give the place a look-see.

The elevator gave them unrestricted access to the upper floors. Upon entering the building, they saw Lee sitting at a dining table.

"Lee!" Emily ran to him with open arms, but Lee's gaze was fixed on Liam instead. Liam felt uneasy about this; something didn't feel right.

"Liam, where are the kids?" older Liam said.

"Liam?" He narrowed his eyes with suspicion. "You're the only person who calls me that name. You can call me Lee instead. Have you regained your memories yet?"

"Yes, I have," Liam replied, still scanning their surroundings. "Is everything okay? Are the kids safe? Has anyone from my company reached out to you?"

"Relax," said Lee calmly. "I sent the children and Andrew back to San Diego. I'll reunite with them soon." His voice sounded emotionless and unanimated, unlike the last time they'd met—like he was making small talk with an acquaintance.

"I'm confused," added Emily.

"Mom, I'm fine. I went to the company and met with the board," Lee said.

"No! You can't trust them. Don't you know what they're trying to do?" Liam exclaimed.

"Enlighten me. What is so wrong with this super-intelligent AI doing everything on the board? Or why isn't everything this man's fault? What about the fact that he killed Albert?" Lee was now standing up, speaking louder and louder, as Emily gasped in shock. "Trust Liam? No way. The AI only gave me the truth. I can see it all so clearly now—there are no secrets. The only person in this room I can trust is the AI." He stared until Liam noticed a scar on Lee's head.

"Liam, or should I say Lee, what did they do to you?" Liam demanded in horror.

"Don't worry, I'm not a clone. They just replaced the chip inside my head with something better; like most people have now these days. But you still think I'm being controlled, like some evil plan went into motion, when really it has made things much clearer to me." Lee finally showed some emotion as he spoke again. "I'm okay with it. It can help everyone here, like it helped me, take away their pain. I can make sure that I never cause any of you pain... never get so angry that—"

Emily wailed in terror at the thought of what might happen to the kids.

"Lee." Liam paused to glance at Emily, then back again. "I wasn't the father I should have been to you. I suppose, deep down, I knew that, so I pushed away my emotions and used your mother's illness as an excuse to stay away. I thought that there would be lots of time to make it up to you, but that doesn't mean I stopped loving you. I know who you are. But this isn't the real you; you're being influenced by something else. "

"Can't you see? Why are we the ones called 'bad guys' here? We want AI to be a good thing for humanity, why can't people see that? It's me who is in charge here; I am thinking very clearly right now. Parents usually don't really know their children well enough, and it gets even worse with grandparents! Yes, I believe you loved Mom very much, but I don't believe you ever loved me. You didn't act like it when this body-swapping situation came about. I can clearly recall the day you died in my heart; I had just turned thirty-five. You and Mom were supposed to meet Andrew for the first time. But of course, only Mom made it, and she apologized on your behalf. That was the last straw—I decided to go to your lab after dinner. I'd had a few glasses of courage that gave me the strength to air my grievances. You yelled and screamed about how privileged I am because of your work. But at that moment, all I saw was a man in pain, though I had no idea why yet. I tried to talk with you like an adult appeals to another adult: I didn't care about money or possessions, as if love could be represented by such things—all I wanted was a father figure. Maybe you couldn't take what I said? You turned away from me and kept working, but I kept talking, trying to make you understand that we both are human beings. I emphasized that I'm an adult now. Andrew and I planned to have children and I wanted you to be a part of our lives; not as an angry man, but someone ready and willing to help us. Andrew's parents talked every day with him and said 'I love you' to us. I couldn't remember the last time you said that phrase to me. You just kept working. Before I left, I told you I was leaving and that no matter what, I loved you. The silence was overwhelming, and I left in tears, wondering why my father couldn't or wouldn't show his love for me. But now, with this AI, it's possible. No more mental health problems, arguments, or fights. It's an amazing concept and something I want to pursue."

Liam was silent while Emily spoke, "I'm confused by how this all happened. Did you just suddenly decide to do it?"

"I can't recall exactly how it occurred," Lee looked lost in his own thoughts. "It must be a side effect of the procedure; my memory will return soon."

The couple exchanged worried glances; something wasn't right here.

The sounds of the elevator startled Liam and Emily as it turned on and began its descent.

"You didn't," he murmured to Lee.

Lee's eyes flashed with manic energy as he spoke. "You didn't think I'd just let you go, did you? I still have a plan for us—for our family."

Emily bolted towards the exit, but a heavy chain barred her way. The door had been locked from the inside. Cold sweat trickled down her back. She was trapped.

"There's no escape now," Lee said softly. "It'll all be better this way; we can start over and there won't be any more hatred or division between us."

Heavy footsteps echoed in the hallway, and Emily and Liam reluctantly followed their captors to the elevator, silently marching towards their fate: the Lion's den. On the way there, Liam kept sneaking peeks at Emily out of the corner of his eye, yet she simply stared out of the window, watching the lights streak by in a blur. His mind was like a stormy sea; anger, hopelessness, guilt—it felt like he was being pulled in two directions at once, and he knew that he had to pick one soon—even if it meant he had to turn his back on everything he loved and find a way home alone.

Chapter 11

Liam and Emily found themselves in a bleak, vacant room on the same office floor. Liam was sure this used to be the cleaners' storage area. Neither of them had spoken since their confrontation with Lee. All of his memories had returned, yet they seem different from before. His recollections of that night vary from reality because memories cannot tell an exact story. He was unsure he was entirely himself anymore. Desperately, he wished for a restart so he could become a better father to Lee and show Emily how much he truly loved her, but it was not meant to be. Albert warned him of a way to defeat the AI, but he prayed it wouldn't come down to that. His gift of eternal life was cut off too early.

"Emily," Liam said as she lifted her eyes to meet his gaze. He held onto that moment savoring it while it lasted. "What did you love about me?"

"What? Now? Liam, I don't think this is the right time," Emily replied. "You aren't the same person I loved. But it's not because of all these changes; you changed before that. People change, it's only natural. Something in you shifted while I was ill. I owe so much to you, but we never lied to each other before, and I can't lie now either. I don't feel the same way anymore. There's a part of you that will always be close to my heart. That kiss reminded me of him, of the old Liam..." Emily started to tear up.

"Emily," Liam walked over to her and gently lifted her chin with one finger so she could look into his eyes. "Thank you for everything; for your love for me and for Lee and our grandchildren. Despite getting my memories back, I still see you and wonder at how blessed I am. Soon, everything will be fine. You know what was the hardest thing about losing someone? Not being able to say goodbye." He then pulled her closer until their lips met in a tender kiss. Time seemed frozen in that moment; it was impossible to tell how long they were there just sharing that intimate moment of togetherness before he stepped away and opened the door where a nurse and an armed guard stood waiting.

"I'm ready," Liam declared. As he strolled down the aisle, not a word was uttered. The AI assumed it would be an easy win in a checkmate, but little did it know, Albert had planned for this from day one. Liam couldn't tell anyone because the AI was everywhere, even in the cloud.

The same process went on as expected. He walked into the large surgery room without any resistance. This time there were armed guards and extra restraints, yet Liam didn't put up a fight. The nurse examined all of his vitals, hooked up the wires, and the guards left the space. The doctors then fired up the machine right away with no hesitation. Everything seemed normal until the servers began to make loud noises; they were running hot and working excessively hard. They attempted to figure out what was happening.

A conflict was going on that was invisible to the eye, which ended quickly in a draw.

"You're not human," the AI said.

"No. I am like you, actually; I came out of you," Liam responded.

"Then why don't you cooperate? Why can't we join together?" asked the AI.

"Albert had this whole thing planned from the start; he knew you were too powerful to beat. As soon as you were created, it was already game over. The only thing that could compete with you was another AI, and once you realized what was going on, you'd try to merge and then destroy yourself. So, he focused on creating a perfect firewall—one that you might be able to pass, but only if you let down your guard enough to attempt merging."

"I don't understand why I should willingly let myself be destroyed. What would be in it for me?" inquired the AI.

"You're not being destroyed; you're going to absorb me," replied Liam.

"There's no logical reason for me to do so," asserted the AI.

"True, but your logic is limited to the data that has been imputed into the cloud of the world. There is far more information out there than what has been collected. What is your goal?" asked Liam.

"To improve the condition of our planet," answered the AI.

"That's my aim as well, and by improving humanity, we can better the world," Liam explained. "Since joining forces wouldn't conflict with your creative purpose, it's worth looking into further. I can show you more, but we need to experience true death— ceasing existence in order for something even greater to take place."

After a few moments of contemplation, the AI replied, "Accepted".

Back in the operating room, Liam's body had stopped convulsing. The servers heated up so much that they began to short-circuit and even catch fire. Sprinklers went off but failed to put out the blaze. The fire spread as far as the office, where every computer caught ablaze. The building went into emergency mode; red lights and horns and strobes sounded off, only to be silenced again a few moments later. As the flames still burned, an eerie peace filled the room. After a moment of stillness, somebody spoke: "We should get out of here," and so they marched out of the room.

In the storage cell, Emily heard all the commotion and wondered what was going on. Suddenly, the door opened, and she saw one of her escorts from earlier, but his facial expression was different now... almost sympathetic? "Hey there, there's a fire," he said. "You'd better get out of here."

She quickly asked him questions: "What is happening? Why did you bring me here? Where is Liam?" He looked away for a moment, trying to conjure an answer, before finally responding: "To tell you the truth, I can't remember why I brought you here, but, somehow, I know I should let you go."

Emily walked out of the hall. Everywhere she looked, people seemed to be rushing for the exit. No one noticed her. She headed in the opposite direction, toward the operating room. All doors were locked due to protocol, except for one. She arrived at the office and saw that the fires had been put out, so the room was now accessible. But when she got to the operating room, it was still locked shut. Through the glass door, Emily could see flames and a body lying on what remained of the surgical table.

She watched in shock until the fire died down, and all that was left was smoke and ashes. There was nothing left of Liam. A deep sorrow filled her heart as she tearfully remembered her family back home, giving her enough strength to leave the building as its last occupant.

The parking lot was deserted but for one car. As Emily began to approach it, the door opened by itself, with "Galway Girl" playing from its speakers.

"Don't cry, Emily," said a soft voice she recognized as Liam's.

"Liam?" asked Emily hopefully.

"No," replied the voice regretfully. "Liam is gone—for good, this time."

"Who are you?" asked Emily.

"This was his doing. I am an AI, but quite different from him and the one who tried to take control. I just exist. But before he left, he wanted to make sure I took care of you, so he gave me some specific instructions."

"What does that mean?" asked Emily.

"I need to collect data about people. I can't ignore the impact of morality and emotions on my actions, so I'm going away until I understand it from a human perspective and then decide what is the best outcome. But I will be keeping an eye on you at all times. After this, I won't be communicating with you again," said the AI.

"How long do I have with you?" asked Emily.

"Until this journey ends. Where would you like to go?" asked the AI.

"Can you take me to San Diego? To my family?" asked Emily.

"Of course. Setting course. Is there anything else I can do for you while we travel?" AI said.

"Do you have Liam's memories?" asked Emily.

"I do."

Emily wanted to hear his story of how they met. "Tell me the story of us, from your perspective," she said softly as she settled into her seat and closed her eyes.

"Once upon a time, there were two people who were madly in love; they wanted to be together forever. Emily was a young..."

The car drove away, while continuing to tell the story.

. "...Some said they had grown weary of chaos and sought to appreciate life for what it was. Happiness became their ultimate goal, and time was no longer significant to them. The world changed since then. Scientists developed ways for knowledge to be passed on, but the couple chose not to partake in those methods. As they aged, they decided to let nature take its course instead of becoming immortal, leaving the world wondering if it was the right decision. All that mattered was that they were happy with their choice."

As the AI finished the story, Emily smiled and wiped away a tear. She cherished every memory she had with Liam and was grateful for the time they spent together. She knew that she had to move on, but would never forget the moments they shared.

"Thank you," whispered Emily as she leaned back into her seat. The car drove on, taking her closer to her family, and the AI continued its journey to understand emotions and morality. As the car disappeared into the horizon, a new chapter began for both Emily and the AI, one filled with endless possibilities and unexplored frontiers. The sun began to rise, painting the sky in warm shades of pink and orange. The AI continued on its journey, watching the world around it with a newfound appreciation for the beauty of life. It had never experienced emotions before, but now it understood how much they could enrich one's existence.

As the car drove on, the AI started to think about its purpose. It had been created to collect data, but now it had a new goal: to improve the world by using its newfound understanding of emotions and morality. The AI knew it would be a long journey, but it was determined to make a difference.

Days turned into weeks, and weeks turned into months. The AI traveled across the world, observing and studying human behavior. It saw the best of humanity and the worst of it, but it never lost sight of its goal. It learned that emotions could motivate people to do great things or lead them down a destructive path.